SOLO STAN

Talia Tucker

Kokila

KOKILA
An imprint of Penguin Random House LLC
1745 Broadway, New York, New York 10019

First published in the United States of America by Kokila,
an imprint of Penguin Random House LLC, 2025

Copyright © 2025 by Talia Tucker

Penguin Random House values and supports copyright. Copyright fuels creativity, encourages diverse voices, promotes free speech, and creates a vibrant culture. Thank you for buying an authorized edition of this book and for complying with copyright laws by not reproducing, scanning, or distributing any part of it in any form without permission. You are supporting writers and allowing Penguin Random House to continue to publish books for every reader. Please note that no part of this book may be used or reproduced in any manner for the purpose of training artificial intelligence technologies or systems.

Kokila & colophon are registered trademarks of Penguin Random House LLC.
The Penguin colophon is a registered trademark of Penguin Books Limited.

Visit us online at PenguinRandomHouse.com.

Library of Congress Cataloging-in-Publication Data
Names: Tucker, Talia, author. | Title: Solo Stan / by Talia Tucker.
Description: New York, New York: Kokila, 2025. | Summary: Two solo concertgoers, Kai and Elias, share a romantic summer night together when the concert is cut short by a blackout.
Identifiers: LCCN 2024052376 (print) | LCCN 2024052377 (ebook) | ISBN 9780593624784 (hardcover) | ISBN 9780593624807 (epub) | Subjects: CYAC: Summer romance—Fiction. | Concerts—Fiction. | LGBTQ+ people—Fiction. | African Americans—Fiction. | LCGFT: Romance fiction. | Novels.
Classification: LCC PZ7.1.T8225 So 2025 (print) | LCC PZ7.1.T8225 (ebook) | DDC [Fic]—dc23
LC record available at https://lccn.loc.gov/2024052376
LC ebook record available at https://lccn.loc.gov/2024052377

ISBN 9780593624784

1 3 5 7 9 10 8 6 4 2

Printed in the United States of America
BVG

This book was edited by Joanna Cárdenas, copyedited by Bethany Bryan, proofread by Rachel Skelton, and designed by Asiya Ahmed. The production was supervised by Rye White, Madison Penico, Natalie Vielkind, Misha Kydd, and Lisa Schwartz.

Text set in ABC Marist

This book is a work of fiction. Any references to historical events, real people, or real places are used fictitiously. Other names, characters, places, and events are products of the author's imagination, and any resemblance to actual events or places or persons, living or dead, is entirely coincidental.

The publisher does not have any control over and does not assume any responsibility for author or third-party websites or their content

The authorized representative in the EU for product safety and compliance is Penguin Random House Ireland, Morrison Chambers, 32 Nassau Street, Dublin D02 YH68, Ireland, https://eu-contact.penguin.ie.

To me, for always being that b— Well, you know.

KAI

Dakarai had always been curious about what it would be like to date himself and why no one else ever seemed to want to. As he stood outside a bright yellow retro theater flowerless, slightly hungry, and having opened all his own doors that evening, he couldn't say he recommended it.

Dakarai, or Kai as he preferred, bit the inside of his lip, and his throat felt dry as he looked up at the marquee:

> THE HERITAGE PLAYHOUSE PRESENTS
> **CYPHR**
> SOLD OUT

Excited concertgoers filed in below, illuminated by the glittering Hollywood bulbs of the theater's entrance, all dressed well enough to take the stage themselves.

As Kai joined them, he suddenly had the air knocked from his lungs by someone going against the current.

"You need tickets?" the someone asked in lieu of an apology.

Kai raised an eyebrow at the scalper.

Tickets weren't his problem—he'd started with four: for him; his best friend, Bobby; Bobby's girlfriend, Winter; and Winter's best friend, Emmy. He'd purchased them online and not from *a guy* in a trench coat, like Kai's father said he used to do in "the good ol' days." But now Kai only needed one after his friends had informed him that they would no longer be in town for the concert—or, in fact, the entire summer.

"You selling better friends?" Kai muttered to the scalper, brushing himself off, though it was unlikely that replacements for the three traitors could fit up the grifter's sleeve.

Bypassing the line into the theater, the tech-averse Kai flashed his paper ticket, the only one in a sea of scannable digital tickets. The red-carpeted stairs led him to a cozy, dimly lit area. He found his seat, number twelve in the front row, and settled in. Seat eleven next to him remained empty.

Another solo attendee, perhaps? he thought.

As the rest of the theater lights flickered, signaling that the concert was about to start, the openers—two female rappers who had recently gone viral on TikTok—charged from backstage and launched into their performance without introduction. The audience swelled as the crowd rose to their feet and screamed their throats raw. Kai rose as well, unconcerned that his six-foot-five frame would ruin the experience of those behind him. He had, after all, paid just like anyone else. And it seemed that his friends, his new coworker at the bookstore, and perhaps the entire universe, were all trying to ruin his last summer before college. He was determined to have fun, even if it was purely out of spite. In fact, he wished there was a spotlight on him right then so everyone could see just how happy he was to be alone at the show. This was a new season of Kai. A reboot. It was solo summer. Selfish summer. The summer of Dakarai.

Any inhibitions he had left were gone when CYPHR walked

out onto the stage, leather pants clinging to his slender frame, a white tank top stretched out around his neck, exposing several tattoos scattered across his chest and down both arms. He had well-defined features and expressive large brown eyes that were hooded by a heavy brow line. When CYPHR looked up, Kai could finally see his face clearly on the screen that backlit his form.

"Who in here knows a little band called EZF? If you're a Dropout, make some noise!" CYPHR yelled into the mic. The crowd roared. Then CYPHR put his fingers to his lips, and everyone instantly hushed. Teachers wished they could have this power. CYPHR continued in a softer tone, "Now, who in here has no idea what I'm talking about and came here just for me?"

The small venue became one loud scream.

CYPHR made a winding gesture in the air, a signal to his band. When Kai's favorite song started, his indignant determination to have fun gave way to genuine enjoyment. Making use of the empty space next to him, he danced and sang out of tune with everyone else.

> ♪ *If we kiss once, we can't take it back*
> *But if we kiss this once, I can kiss you again*
> *Let's make another mistake*
> *The first mistake is already made* ♪

Preoccupied, Kai didn't notice that someone had come down his row until they were almost in front of him. Their face was hidden beneath a black bucket cap, and the stage backlit them in a way that darkened their features. This was the person who had bought seat eleven from him only hours ago. Kai was intrigued yet slightly disappointed as he anticipated having to shrink his range of motion—and therefore the sincere pleasure he had finally found being alone.

Before Seat Eleven could sit, an amp blew out, releasing a feedback loop that pierced through the theater and caused everyone to collectively clap their hands over their ears. Startled, Seat Eleven stumbled on a purse on the ground, and Kai instinctively reached out, catching them by the arm before they fell over the loge-level balcony. The screech ceased as quickly as it had punctuated the air, and Kai's focus shifted entirely to the stranger's chipped black nails digging into his skin, the electricity of the moment passing back and forth between them within the conduit of their touch.

As though irritated that they had just been saved from having accidental floor seats, the stranger brusquely pushed Kai away, waking him up to the commotion surrounding them.

Kai was unaware of what his body was doing. He wasn't even sure if he was breathing. But if he'd been smiling, it dropped right off his face the moment Seat Eleven finally looked up so Kai could see who was under the bucket cap.

The person he saw was striking, sharp and pristine, as if cut into existence with a blade. They turned their head to the side, clearly embarrassed, revealing an angular jaw that seemed unaccustomed to smiling.

Kai's mind went blank as the ringing persisted in his ears. All he could manage to say was "What the fuck?"

2
ELIAS

One Week Ago

Elias was lying on his bed, flat on his face, wondering if staying there any longer would cause him to dematerialize and fall through the mattress. It was a hot, humid day in New York City, and there was no part of his body that wanted to move even a millimeter. The open windows teased him; the air outside was just as hot, like a warm breath from the underbelly of the city.

Elias cast his gaze to the other side of the room at a neatly made bed. It'd been unslept in for the past few weeks.

This was the extent of his post–high school plan. He thought that maybe he and his twin brother would try to start a business together, or perhaps move somewhere with turquoise beaches and fewer people. The two of them had been in New York all their lives and had always talked about seeing more of the world. William decided to see the world without him by way of the US Navy. They'd written to each other as often as they could, but the letters abruptly stopped one day. The last one read:

Hey Eli,
   Hope you're good. Miss you. But I got to say, your last

letter stung. Mom and Dad are going to do what they're going to do, and Nia's not a kid anymore. Maybe things weren't like this before, but now it feels like you're the one needing us more than we need you. I didn't abandon the family. I found a place for myself over here. Maybe it's your turn to do the same. You're a few minutes older than I am, but you're not my big brother.

—William

Sliding the letter under his pillow for the hundredth time, Elias looked up at the popcorn ceiling and sank into his thoughts.

Without William, Elias's future felt uncertain. Despite his lengthy in-school and out-of-school suspension record, Elias was a decent student. Yet, college still didn't seem like the right path. He graduated with a class of about seventy-five other kids, most of whom only went to college to prove something to their parents. Others joined the military, some got jobs at supermarkets or delivering food, and some did nothing at all. Because the class was so small, everyone knew everyone else's business. When they all found out William was joining the military, everyone assumed Elias would do the same.

Flailing his arms and legs to wrestle his way out of a tangle of sheets, Elias finally decided to direct his anger at his hair. His fingers found the edge of the bed, and he swung his legs to the side. In a few steps, he reached the bathroom.

His short hair had been bleached a pale gold by William. The color suited him for a while, but he had overgrowth of dark roots and no William to redo it for him.

With unsteady hands, Elias grabbed the clippers from the

drawer and clicked them on. He carefully began sculpting his hair down to its natural black. The clippers jammed, so Elias slammed his hand against the back of them. Despite the loud noise, it wasn't doing anything. He cursed under his breath when he hit them too hard and the front cover popped off and cracked on the floor, leaving him 50 percent blond and 100 percent over everything.

"Lord, I see what you have done for others. When will it be my turn?" Elias muttered to the ceiling, expelling an exasperated breath.

Elias's little sister, Nia, poked her head into the bathroom. Her hands gripped the doorframe, which had thick layers of cracking plasticky paint. Years of weather fluctuations caused the old wood to shrink and expand and the paint to separate like a molting skin.

"Favorite big brother," Nia said in a singsong voice, "you busy?"

"Don't do that," Elias replied. "What do you want?"

"Luis invited me to play basketball with him and some other people. Can you come with me?"

"It's too hot. Just take your phone with you. I'm here," he said, picking up the broken piece of the razor. As soon as he began to correct his error of not closing the bathroom door in the first place, the unmistakable sound of their mother bickering with their father on the phone in the other room reached him. A heavy exhale escaped him, and he opened the door again. "Actually, I would literally do anything to get out of this house, but I can't go outside looking like this," he said, pointing to his half-shaven hair.

Nia folded her arms. "I thought Nike Panda was the look you were going for."

"You always got something to say. Just help me!" Elias whined, satisfied when the thick bathroom door and the buzzing of the razor

Nia had repaired were enough to drown out his mother's agitated voice.

Grabbing his keys and phone, Elias yelled to their mother that he was going out with Nia. He groaned all the way down the six flights of stairs while Nia hopped down them in twos. When he reached the stoop outside the building, he paused to admire the blue sky, partially obscured by the tall New York City walk-ups.

"Nia, you're late! Come on!" Luis yelled from the court.

As Elias approached with Nia, the other players instinctively retreated; the atmosphere noticeably shifted, silently acknowledging his presence. Their eyes bored into him, an unspoken fact lingering—he wasn't wanted there, precisely why Nia always brought him. They played more fairly when he was around. He was used to it, but these little boys needed to learn respect quickly if they were going to continue playing with his little sister.

Nia tossed Elias her bag and charged toward the open court.

"Ignore them. They're just worried about getting beat by a girl," Luis said, placing a hand on Nia's back. "Let's play."

Elias pretended to be engrossed in his phone, but his eyes never left the game. Nia threw a high-arching shot that smacked against the backboard then bounced across the pavement. A few of the other boys laughed in a gloating manner. Elias tried his best to remain calm, even though the heat was causing him to boil over quicker than usual.

Elias shot to his feet at the sudden clang of the chain-link fence. One of the players, Connor, had angrily slammed the ball against it and yelled, "Stop grabbing on my shirt!" at Nia.

"Don't touch her," Elias warned.

"Because she's a girl I have to go easy on her?" Connor retorted.

"No, you should go easy on her because she'll lay your little dumb ass out and I'll pretend like I didn't see anything."

"Whatever," Connor said, throwing the ball roughly at Nia, who narrowly caught it.

Luis put his body between Elias and Connor, but Elias easily evaded him. He shoved Connor in the chest and then stood over him, looking down with disdain. "Get your weight up, little boy," Elias said, his nostrils flaring.

"Get my weight up? Get your age down, old man," Connor replied, slipping the grasp of the others.

Connor grabbed Elias by the front of his shirt, and Elias panicked. Realizing he couldn't fight a thirteen-year-old, he raised his hands in a too-little-too-late gesture of surrender. *Fuck,* he thought as he felt the bite from Connor's fist against the side of his nose like an electric surge through his body. Elias was thrown off-balance and crashed into Luis, his head ringing like a church bell. The red-hot pain radiated in his face. Everything went white for a moment, and Elias laughed at his own stupidity as his mouth filled with blood from his gushing nose.

From the corner of his eye, all he saw was the orange blur of the basketball whizzing through the air. It collided with Connor's stomach, creating a resounding *smack*. The impact caused him to stumble backward. Nia then forcefully pushed Connor aside.

"Let's go," she urged, taking a firm grasp on Elias's arm.

"Are there seriously no girls you can play with instead of these little assholes?" Elias asked, spitting blood onto the ground.

"I promise they'd hit you a lot harder."

"I know you know that's not what I meant."

As they left the court, the boys began to argue, their harsh words echoing across the street. Elias's admiration for Luis deepened as he defended Nia's right to play with them. Clearly, Luis had a crush on Nia, but Elias's little sister was completely oblivious. What Elias couldn't figure out, however, was why *his* face was the one to suffer for it.

"You didn't have to do that," Nia said as they ascended the stairs.

He wiped his nose on the inside of his shirt. "I know."

"You're going to get in trouble again if Mom and Dad find out."

"I know."

Nia leaned her head against Elias's arm. "Thanks."

When they reached the apartment, Elias headed to the bathroom and splashed water on his face for relief. Blood that was thinned by the water dripped from his split lip. He reached for some blue mouthwash and swirled it around. When he spat it out, it was tinted pink.

Elias returned to his room, where he threw himself onto the bed, getting droplets of blood on the sheets. He turned over, and his eyes fell on his reflection in the mirror sitting on his bedside table. He got only a moment's reprieve before a forceful knock boomed at his door, a sound he recognized too well—one that told him he'd fucked up. *Again.* He'd left bloodied tissues in the bathroom, so he knew it wouldn't be long before he got that knock.

As the door creaked open, he braced himself for the upcoming lecture. His face was rigid, a mixture of apathy and defiance.

"If it isn't Cassius Clay in his prime," Dad teased, aiming a few air punches at Elias's stomach. "Except Nia told me you folded like Cassius Play-Doh."

Elias stared blankly at his father. "Go ahead and get the lecture over with."

"All right, now, Salty Ray Robinson, take it easy. I'm messin' with you."

"Did you come here just to make jokes?" Elias asked. He covered his face with his arm.

"I'm here to pick up your sister," Dad replied. "It's my weekend."

"You're not helping." Mom had appeared in the doorway, and she was talking to Elias's father. "Just go get Nia ready. I'll handle this."

Elias's father resigned easily, leaving the room to help Nia gather her things.

Being eighteen, Elias no longer had to go with Nia. He hated to leave his mother alone in the apartment now that William was gone too. But feeling the heat of his mother's rage, Elias nearly called his father back to save him.

"This was your last chance, Eli," Mom said resolutely. "You're going to live with your uncle in North Carolina. We've talked about this before, and your father and I agree it'd be the best thing for you."

Elias kept his face covered. "You're not even going to let me explain what happened?"

"I put too much trust in you," she replied, completely ignoring him. He might as well have not even been in the room. "This is all my fault."

"Oh my God. Please, don't be a martyr. This is clearly Dad's fault," he said with a half-hearted smile. He hadn't drawn in enough air to laugh, so it came out in sputters.

"You're joking at a time like this? You *are* just like him."

The blood rushed out of Elias's head as he sat up too quickly, putting stars in his eyes. "How many times have I asked you not to say stuff like that to me? Can't you and Dad be normal and ground me?"

"We—" she began.

"No, you can't," Elias interrupted, "because who would pick Nia up from school and make dinner when you're working nights at the hospital?"

Mom released a weary breath. "I don't have the energy to argue with you, Eli. Please, just get your things ready. You'll be leaving this week."

"What are you going to do without me here?"

"We'll manage. Worry about yourself."

KAI

Three Days Ago

Pop sat on the softest part of the sofa, his eyes fixed on the news. This was his nightly routine. He would get himself feeling as terrible as he could right before dinner so he could have a reason to thank God for the meal he was about to put into his mouth.

Kai went into the kitchen to help his mother.

Mama was standing over a bubbling pot of pureed roasted vegetables, stirring it with her favorite wooden spoon. Kai snuck past her, took a few ladles of the sauce, and poured them over a bowl of rice before Mama dumped the oxtails in. He watched as she stirred the bony cuts of meat. They created a clacking sound against her spoon that made Kai wince.

"Don't you make that face at my cooking," Mama said. She would have hit him with the spoon if it wouldn't put her white counters at risk.

"You know I got love for you, Mama. It's the meat," he replied.

"I don't know how you got so tall eating nothing. You need to learn how to cook if you're going to be so picky. Or at least find a wife who will do it for you."

"Or husband."

Mama tutted. "Then there will be two unsatisfied men in your marriage."

Kai leaned against the refrigerator. "Animals in distress are full of hormones and chemicals that will go into your body," he said. "When you eat meat, you're tasting their last moments."

"You're about to taste *your* last moments if you don't stop putting fingerprints on my appliances, and why are your toes out in my kitchen?" Mama said, all in one breath.

Kai looked down at his bare feet. "You're cooking a pot full of bones that come from a cow batty, and you're worried about my feet?"

"Get your toes out of my kitchen and take your mouth with you."

Kai laid out plates and silverware on the table. He smoothed down the cracking plastic cover over the polished wood he hadn't seen since the table was purchased almost a decade ago. The place where Mama usually sat was in the worst shape because her bangles hit the edge when she ate.

Everyone sat down, and Pop made a production out of saying grace. He grew up in Louisiana and always joked that he was born with a Bible in his hand. He thanked and blessed everyone and everything down to the shoes he wore to get him to the table.

Kai was almost too tired to eat by the time the *amen* came, and every time he chewed, he could feel his new braids tugging at his scalp on the side that was done.

"Stop playing with your hair," Pop warned.

"You got a little follicle envy, Pop?" Kai said with a low chuckle.

"If hair was so important, it wouldn't grow in some of the places that it does." Pop's voice was stern, but his hand went straight for his shaved head. The water in Pop's glass rippled as he returned his hand to it, gripping the cup protectively as though someone would steal it away.

"Don't be nasty, Reggie," Mama said, lightly smacking Pop with the back of her hand. Pop winked at her, and the briefest of smiles passed over Mama's face.

They fell into silence, and Kai watched his parents eat. They picked up the bones with their hands and spun them around in their mouths like washing machines until the bones were clean. Kai could hear the clicks and pops and tuts of their lips and teeth producing a language he had unfamiliarized himself with years ago. When Kai was nine, he received the bicycle he still rode around to that day as a Christmas present. It was a bright red cruiser with whitewalls and chrome handlebars. He and Bobby rode it around the neighborhood during the heart of winter when the outside didn't call for bike riding or Rollerblading or sitting on stoops. But he had wanted to try it. He ran right off the curb, hit a mailbox, and heard one of the bones in his arm crack like wood.

He never ate meat again.

With Kai's stomach still rumbling, Mama cleared away the plates, leaving Pop to wash the dishes alone. He hummed softly to himself as he filled the dishwasher.

Kai settled on the floor of the living room, positioning himself in front of Mama. She absentmindedly tugged at his hair while watching the news Pop had abandoned on the TV. Kai rested his head on Mama's knee and looked on with her, sideways.

Pop brought a hot towel for Mama to place over Kai's head when she was done. She gently arranged it over the tight braids and massaged with as much tenderness as she could manage. The feeling enveloped Kai's entire body, and he closed his eyes, settling into a half sleep.

"You baby that boy too much, you know," Pop said quietly as he took a seat on the other side of the couch.

"I know," Mama replied, her voice warm and soothing.

A hush fell over them, and for a while, the sound of the television was all that could be heard.

Kai kept his eyes closed, leaving his head leaning against his mother's leg as he idly listened to the local news. It was the same old routine—accidents causing traffic jams, a local man opening a pizza shop and donating most of his proceeds to animal shelters, and some entertainment news about old celebrities Kai had never heard of—until his ears perked up at the sound of a familiar name.

"North Carolina native artist CYPHR, formerly of the band EZF, recently launched his solo career and has announced a surprise show this Friday in Raleigh. Tickets are currently available. You can visit our website for more information," the newscaster announced.

With those words, Kai leapt to his feet, kissed his parents on the cheeks, and climbed the stairs to his bedroom in three long steps. He flopped backward onto his bed and had smoke in the air and his nose in his phone before his head even touched the pillow.

His phone was a relic, so it took many minutes of nail biting and buffering until he got the confirmation that his purchase for four tickets had gone through. He, Bobby, Winter, and Emmy would be seeing CYPHR that weekend whether they liked it or not.

He closed the page and immediately called Bobby.

Bobby answered the phone as though they had already been mid-conversation. "I'm just going to say it. Being a boyfriend is stressful. Especially Winter Park's boyfriend. Ten out of ten, would not recommend."

"Well, you did go back on your promise to go to Harvard, randomly deciding to haul your ass to the other side of the country," Kai countered as he settled onto the bed.

"Whose side are you on?"

Kai let out a chuckle.

Bobby and Winter liked to pretend they hated each other, but Kai felt the heat of their unspoken connection, the invisible red thread that bound Bobby and Winter together. He was certain they were twin flames—two halves of a single soul reunited. A twin flame connection was a spiritual one that could shift your life and worldview in profound ways. Meeting this person was about more than just love; it could open your eyes to the divine, push you to strive for higher consciousness, and ignite a passion to become a more enlightened soul all around. This type of deep, meaningful bond wasn't necessarily romantic in nature, but Kai hoped that when he found his own twin flame, it would be.

"Whatever, dude. I didn't call to talk about your relationship problems. I called to ask what you're doing on Friday," Kai said, unable to contain his excitement any longer.

"I, uh—actually have to talk to you about that," Bobby said. "I know we're supposed to spend the whole summer together—me, you, and Emmy, but—"

"Robert Bae, what did you do?" Kai asked sternly.

"I may have gotten a summer internship."

"No . . ."

"In California."

"Bruh . . ."

"And I leave in three days."

Kai sat up straight. "What?! When did you find out about this?"

"I was wait-listed, and I guess someone dropped out last minute. They called me yesterday."

"And you're only telling me now?"

"Well, I couldn't deal with both you and Winter being mad at me in one day." Bobby went silent for a moment. "You're not saying anything. What were you going to ask me to do on Friday?"

Kai shuffled around in his blankets before rolling onto his stomach. "How long is the internship?" he asked, avoiding the question.

"All summer—then I'll immediately start at Berkeley in the fall."

Anxious, Kai twirled his barbell earring between his fingertips. He tried to change the subject again by asking, "Have you apologized to Winter yet? I hate when you guys fight."

"I sent her a bushel of apples."

Kai took a moment to process. "You did what?"

"In Korean, *apple* and *apology* are the same word. I don't know—I thought it'd be cute!" Bobby's tone grew more defensive with each word.

"Boy, if you don't apologize the right way," Kai said, clicking his tongue against his teeth. "Y'all always fight over the stupidest stuff. Last time, it was because you put butter in the refrigerator. The time before that, it was because Winter watches movies with the subtitles on. The time before that, it was because you bought her mint chocolate chip ice cream. This is a real issue you're having, so stop with the apples, check your pride, and beg for forgiveness."

"You took her side last time too," Bobby huffed.

"Because you told her you don't like Meryl Streep!" Kai said, exasperated.

Bobby let out an airy laugh. "All right, all right! I'll apologize."

"She and Emmy are probably free on Friday, though, right? I'm sure they'll just complain about you the entire time."

"Well . . ." Bobby began.

"Now what?"

"Winter was just so mad, I asked her to come with me. And—"

"There's an *and*?!"

"Well, now that Winter won't be here this summer, Emmy isn't coming back to the States after all."

Kai's body completely deflated. "You guys are really leaving me all alone this summer?"

"I know, but this internship could really help me get a leg up," Bobby said with a deep sigh. "And I was mad at you first. Don't UNO-reverse me."

"What are you mad at *me* for?" Kai asked with an incredulous snort.

"*You're* the one who's leaving *me* all alone. We were supposed to go to Berkeley together, remember? We were going to get an apartment. I already bought us a friendship ficus."

Kai's brow furrowed in confusion. "What's a friendship ficus?"

"A ficus between friends. Now it's just a regular ficus."

"Well, you were going to let me move to California! You know I'm not ready for something like that!"

"It was *your* idea!" The frustration was evident in Bobby's voice.

It had been Kai's idea, in fact. But then he pictured himself on the West Coast, away from his family, pursuing a career in tech and UX design when he didn't even own a smartphone. The entire idea was half-baked, so he elected to stay home instead, even at the risk of being a townie.

"Sorry," Kai responded, his tone devoid of any genuine remorse.

"Wow, you could do better than that."

"I'll send you an apple. I gotta go," Kai said, feeling suddenly panicky. "Love you, Bae!"

"The only apple you need is an iPhone!" Bobby managed to say before Kai snapped his phone shut.

Kai closed his eyes and put on headphones, but he was restless. Typically, he had no trouble falling asleep, but after having all his summer plans shattered in one phone call, his mind was in too many places. He sat quietly at the edge of his bed for a moment before deciding he needed to get outside. Perhaps a bike ride would clear his head.

Kai's bicycle tires kicked up little water droplets as he rode across the damp grass to get to Uncle Moodie's Books, where he'd been working for the last year.

When Kai walked in, his nose was immediately filled with the strong scent of coffee beans mingling with the faint aroma of printed pages. A smile spread across his face. Uncle Moodie's Books was part coffee shop, part bookstore. When you first walked in, rows of comic books brightly displayed alongside collectible action figures lined the right side. To the left, a few bistro tables sat in front of the large cashier counter, which also served as a coffee bar complete with a pastry case. Directly behind the counter was a multipurpose staff room that functioned as a kitchen, office, and break room, with a spacious closet for storage and stock. It was the perfect spot to do inventory in peace or prepare drinks and food away from the customers' eyes.

The jingling bell above the door alerted Kai's boss, the enigmatic Uncle Moodie, to Kai's arrival. His eyes crinkled at the corners as he acknowledged Kai's presence. He was hairless except for a full salt-and-pepper beard and mustache as he clung on to the last of his thirties.

"You're late, young buck," Uncle Moodie said as Kai unhooked his helmet and placed it on the counter. "D&D Night just ended."

"You know I'm not here for a shift, Big Mood," Kai replied, giving a sidelong glance. "I just wanted to see what you got into when I'm not around."

"So that's why you're not going to Hollywood? And here I thought you were sticking around for my famous pies."

"Berkeley isn't Hollywood, Mood," Kai replied, settling on a tall stool as Uncle Moodie fetched him a slice of his *famous* peanut butter pie and matcha hot chocolate with extra gelatin-free marshmallows. Exactly how Kai liked it.

Uncle Moodie wiped his hands on his apron before he reached to close the dessert case door. But as he pushed it, the faulty door caught an obstacle, refusing to budge any farther. He muttered obscenities under his breath as he gave the door another firm tug. Despite his efforts, the door remained jammed, and he let out a sigh.

"I knew you couldn't manage without me, Mood," Kai said with a twinge of pride as he took a bite of pie.

Uncle Moodie wiped his brow. "Can you do repairs?"

"No, sir," Kai replied honestly. He was never good with his hands. Mama always said that his talents were in more highbrow areas, though he wasn't certain how being able to draw the entire cast of *Buffy* from memory was going to help him in situations like this one.

"Hopefully, my nephew Eli's got a few more calluses on his hands than you," Uncle Moodie said with a wry smile. "This ol' place is falling apart, and I'm getting too tired to manage her."

"I'm sure he'll do fine."

Kai didn't even know Uncle Moodie had a nephew until recently, but the nephew was staying for the summer to help out in the store.

Leaning against the counter, Uncle Moodie rested his head in his hand. "Why did you really stop by?" he asked.

"I don't know," Kai answered, wiping the foam from his mouth with his fingertips. He wrapped his arms around himself and shifted back and forth. "I thought I was spending the summer with my friends, but now it looks like you'll be my only friend. I guess it's settling in that they'll really be gone. I knew I'd miss them, but I didn't think it'd feel so much like getting left behind."

"You can still go to Berkeley, can't you?"

"Probably, but I don't think I could handle going that far."

Uncle Moodie's eyes softened. "What do *you* have to be afraid of?"

Kai's boss was almost half a foot shorter than he was. Uncle Moodie commented on their height difference regularly, so Kai tried to shrink himself, mostly in vain. He had to tilt his neck when he went through certain doorways and duck every time he passed a light fixture. He barely even had to look where he was going anymore. It was like he instinctively knew he would bump his head, so there was a permanent curve in his neck from the world not accommodating him. However, Moodie was gentle with Kai and didn't mean anything by it. He had said the first time they met that it was because there was something small about Kai—that he looked like a little boy who started to grow and forgot to stop.

"I'm not ready to go off to college," Kai said, his rocking picking up pace. "I don't think I'm ready to do anything on my own. I don't even know how to tie my shoes."

Moodie let out a deep breath. "As you get older, there might be moments, even years, when you think you've got everything figured out. But then you start to see maybe you're just pretending because folks are watching. No one knows what they're doing. Don't let anybody ever fool you into thinking they got all the answers. You're a good kid. You'll find your way."

"What if I just stayed right here instead?"

Moodie appeared to contemplate for a moment, probably trying to come up with some answer that would earn him the Uncle Moodie nickname that made him sound old and wise. He grabbed one of the freshly washed mugs and turned it right side up. He filled it with steaming hot water for his tea. "We all have to do things sometimes that we don't want to do," he said. "But growing up means learning when those things are going to help us out in the long term or when we should say no."

"So you're saying I made the right choice in staying home?"

"I'm saying that only you can decide if it's the right choice for you."

Kai blinked rapidly, disguising the glimmer of tears with a quick smile as Moodie gave him a few rough slaps on the back.

"Any chance you want to go to a concert on Friday?" Kai asked, disguising a sniffle as a laugh.

"You know I can't stay out late like I used to," Moodie replied.

"Yeah, I'm just kidding. You know I can't be seen out with someone old enough to be my dad," Kai teased.

"Get out of here, boy," Moodie said, tossing the rag he'd been using to clean the counter at Kai. "Wipe them tears and get ready for your shift in a couple days. I need you to train my nephew."

Kai put his hand to his forehead in a salute. "Yes, sir."

"And learn how to tie your damn shoes!"

Returning home, Kai got back into bed. He thought long and hard to himself. As a firm believer in things happening for a reason, there had to be one for why he'd be alone that summer. Maybe with his friends gone, it was a sign he should reach for other connections.

Where am I being guided? Kai thought.

He hoped it was toward love—the real thing this time. He thought about Winter and Bobby, together in California, and Emmy, the extraordinary extrovert she was, with whom he'd had a brief infatuation the previous year, meeting all kinds of new people in Europe, where she was pursuing a modeling career. As he looked up at the ceiling, hearing his parents laughing together down the hall, he was hit with a pang of loneliness.

All his previous romances ended as quickly as they began, sometimes even *before* they began. He had a habit of moving fast when he met people he liked, which he had to admit was often. *More often than I change my socks,* according to Bobby. It didn't take much—a smile, even a simple hello—and he would fall head over heels. He'd lay all his cards on the table, even at the risk of scaring them off, and they would always come up with some excuse as to why they couldn't be in a relationship with him. It was always a lie, just a way to let him down easy. One person said they had recently gotten into K-pop and would be too busy learning the names of the members of NCT to date. Another said their dogs had twins. Another abruptly decided to move to Guam. One had started binge-watching *Law & Order*. And another had recently gotten into competitive air guitar.

For Kai, love always came easily. It was reciprocity that was the issue. There was only one time his feelings turned into an actual relationship, even if it wasn't the kind that he'd initially hoped for.

About five years ago, he had been sitting in the park with

his sketchbook. The only other people there were two brothers, possibly twins, and, presumably, their little sister. One of the brothers kept his eyes firmly glued to his phone, but the other had been fixated on the little girl. Every time any of the other kids even looked like they might bump into her, he leapt to his feet but then slowly sat back down, probably realizing he shouldn't square up with eight-year-olds. Kai sat for a long while, fastening a lock on that moment by committing it to a page in his sketchbook.

When Kai finally worked up the courage to gift the drawing to the brother, the little girl had come waddling over, her laces undone. The boy, without missing a beat, bent low, tied her laces in the blink of an eye, and sent her off again to play. She hadn't even considered the other twin. She clearly had her favorite, and it was obvious why: He had an energy that reminded Kai of home. In that moment, Kai looked down at his own laces, splayed out on the ground. He then tucked them into his shoes and left the drawing crumpled in the park's trash can.

He remembered inviting Bobby over that afternoon to play *Tekken 7* on the PlayStation. They weren't best friends yet; Kai had been in love with Bobby since the moment he sat next to him in Mr. Melton's fourth-grade class and loaned Bobby a pencil. Calling Bobby a friend felt insincere even though their bond was undeniable. At the time, and even now, all Kai wanted was for someone to notice him, to like him first for once. That included Bobby and the boy from the park, who hadn't even looked his way.

He had confided in Bobby that he wanted to find a boyfriend or girlfriend because his parents had been high school sweethearts, and it was a legacy he had always wanted to carry on. They were only in eighth grade at the time, but it felt urgent.

Bobby paused his game, resting the controller on the rug, and casually suggested that Kai go out with him since they did everything else together anyway. This was classic Bobby, practical to a fault. His tone was so casual, as if he were suggesting they order pizza for dinner or go for a walk. Kai choked on a laugh, thinking Bobby was joking, but Bobby repeated the question. "Why don't you go out with me?"

Then, Kai wasn't sure how it happened, but soon he and Bobby were inching toward each other on the living room rug. To this day, he didn't know whether he should consider it his first kiss or not, because it had been over so quickly.

"Good?" Kai had asked, his shoulders tense.

Bobby put a finger to his chin. "Inconclusive."

They got close again, meeting in a real kiss this time. *This isn't so bad,* Kai thought. It was pleasant, even easy, like walking or breathing. *Maybe a little weird,* he considered as Bobby turned his head farther to the side, but still, not bad. Feeling brave, Kai opened his mouth, allowing the kiss to deepen. However, the moment he felt Bobby's tongue on his, tasting the Swedish Fish they'd eaten together earlier that afternoon, Kai's fight-or-flight response kicked in. *DANGER. DANGER. DANGER. Turn back!* his mind screamed. His eyes shot open, only to find Bobby's open as well, his proximity turning him into a cyclops—not the hot Scott Summers kind, but the *my best friend's tongue is in my mouth* kind. They both flew apart.

And that's how Kai realized that Bobby was his best friend and nothing more. They still joked about the kiss to this day.

Kai exhaled in the warmth of his bed and the glow of candlelight. He reached for a piece of parchment and wrote down his desire to find love, folded it toward himself, and sealed it with a kiss. Placing the paper underneath the candle—which was filled with dried lavender and rose petals, along with sprinkles of cinnamon—he spoke his intentions aloud, hoping that someone was listening—someone who believed he deserved love.

ELIAS

One Day Ago

A dull ache in Elias's nose woke him up again. The cut in his lip had closed, but it still throbbed, and his nose was still sore from the fight. Not that it was much of a fight. Elias took one hit from a middle schooler, then folded like an AARP card–carrying lawn chair.

He reached under his shirt and scratched his stomach as he shifted his head to the side, producing a loud cracking sound from his neck. He scoffed when the other side made no noise.

Eyes barely open yet, Elias shuffled to the fridge, appreciating the chill for a moment before gathering everything needed for breakfast—blueberry pancakes, eggs, and bacon. The small kitchen soon filled with the sweet scent of caramelizing blueberries and fluffy pancake batter sizzling in melted butter.

When the last blueberry pancake slid off his spatula onto the stack, he stood back to admire his work. They weren't pretty, but they were Nia's favorite, and they were done, which was all that mattered when his mom came home from a night shift.

Leaning over the sink, he half-consciously chewed on a slice of bacon until he dozed off and it fell from his mouth into the mixing bowl he was supposed to be washing.

"This is Later Elias's problem," he grumbled, leaving the stack of dirty dishes abandoned in the sink.

He trudged to the bathroom, groaning when he realized the door was locked. Steam rose from beneath it. His mother must have snuck in, then hopped right in the shower. She was usually covered in all sorts of biohazards when she got back from work.

Elias retreated to his room to wait until the bathroom was freed up. Five minutes was adequate. Annoyance glued him to his bed for an extra fifteen. He tossed and turned before rolling onto his stomach, away from his brother's side of the room, Elias's suitcases quietly observing him from the corner. He was flying out in only a few short hours to live with his uncle. A few more minutes passed, and there was a *knock, knock, knock* at his bedroom door. He sat up, prepared to face her, but didn't answer. It was universal knowledge to everyone but his mother that a closed door meant *Go away*. After another set of knocks, there she was in the doorway with a shower cap on her head.

"You still need to go to the bathroom? It's free now."

Of course he still needed to go. He hadn't yet learned how to reabsorb his urine. Elias tightened his jaw and said, "Thanks, Mom."

"Thank you for making breakfast. It smells good."

"I didn't do it for you. I made it for Nia."

Mom shook her head. "I hope you realize all this is for your own good," she said. "I just don't know what to do with you anymore. Maybe getting away from here will help you find your way, figure out what you want to do with your life."

"You're going to pretend you care what I want now?" Elias asked defensively.

"Baby, I love you with everything I got, but sometimes you . . .

29

you scare me, you know? You're getting into fights and causing trouble every day now, it seems. I just don't know what else to do. I can't protect you if you keep carrying on, and I can't have this around your sister. You're her big brother, and she looks up to you. *My* big brother can help you—"

"I don't need help. I can handle myself."

"Then act like it!" Elias's mother snapped.

Elias crossed his arms. "What if I don't want to go?"

"Then you can start looking for your own place to live, because it sure as hell won't be here."

"I'll go, but don't expect me to be happy about it."

"You think I'm worried about your happiness? Go fix yourself up." She clicked her tongue against her teeth and continued her tirade down the hallway.

Elias shook his head and finally went to the bathroom. In the dimness, he was gently touching the tender area around his nose when the door swung open and his dad flicked on the lights without warning. Anger immediately rose within Elias as he squinted against the sudden brightness.

"You all packed up to go?" Dad asked, his usually playful tone uncharacteristically serious. "Your mother needs some rest, but I can take you to the airport."

Elias blinked slowly. "Are you trying to get rid of me sooner?"

Dad's body language was neutral. "Eli, no one's trying to get rid of you. You think I want this? I want you here, taking care of your mother and your sister."

Elias let out a deep breath. "Why don't *you* take care of them?" He flattened himself against the wall to get by his father and added, "I'll call a cab."

Nia, braids piled atop her head, came down the hallway, a plate stacked high with syrupy blueberry pancakes in hand. She shoved a forkful into her mouth, chewing contentedly and exposing her dimples, which matched his own.

"Go back to sleep, kid," Elias said gently.

"Don't tell me what to do," she quipped. She leaned in to give him a one-armed hug, but Elias put up his hands in a defensive gesture.

"Chill. You don't know me like that," he said with a laugh.

The smile dropped from his face when he realized his dad was still standing there, and his mom had also stepped into the narrow hallway. Elias unclenched his jaw, but his fists remained tightly balled. He couldn't handle it anymore.

"I'm leaving now," he declared, returning to his room. Perhaps he *had* in fact learned how to reabsorb his urine.

"Do you have everything, baby? Are you sure you don't want us to come to the airport with you?" Mom asked.

"God no," Elias said.

He got dressed as quickly as he could, collected his things, and wheeled his bag down the stairs and out of the apartment building.

Nia came chasing after him. "You're really going to leave without even saying goodbye properly?"

"It's best I just go quietly. I've already made a mess of everything."

"You'll call, right?"

A fleeting smile tugged at the corner of Elias's mouth. "Be good," he said, pulling his sister into a side hug and planting a quick kiss on her forehead. He climbed into the waiting cab, not glancing back as it drove away.

Elias gazed out of the window as the cab cut through an agonizingly trendy neighborhood. You could go antiquing and then step next door and get an authentic deli bagel covered in lox. After you were done with that, you could walk across the street and get Indian food and a Swedish massage.

Elias couldn't wait to leave it all behind.

It wasn't the city he disliked, but rather the people, the culture, the weather, and the accents. He never understood why a city inhabited by people who used *fuck* like a comma drew so many tourists.

North Carolina didn't exactly bring up good memories for him either. The last time he had been there was about five years ago when his parents were going through their divorce. His mother had packed him, Nia, and William into the car and driven them down to her big brother's house, giving their father until they returned to clear out his things and move into his new place. His mother spent most of the time talking to lawyers and crying on Uncle Moodie's shoulder. William mostly kept to himself, talking to all his friends back in New York constantly, because William's method of dealing with things had always been not to deal with them. That left Elias to be the one to try to explain everything to Nia, who was only eight at the time. They'd go to the park, get sick from eating as much junk food as they wanted because no one was there to tell them no, and stay up late. Elias got used to sleeping with the light on since Nia had been afraid. Even now, he found it difficult to be in the complete dark.

Elias hoped that, this time, North Carolina would signal a more positive change for him. Stepping off the plane and onto the tarmac, Elias felt like he was sweating inside of his own skin. Rushing into the airport was all he could do not to spontaneously combust.

At baggage claim, Elias waited for his luggage to reach him, but a woman in front of him grabbed it before he did.

"That's my bag, ma'am," Elias said.

"Well, you should label your stuff. Everyone has a black bag," she said.

Elias's eyes widened. The coffee she was holding was probably her only personality trait. He wondered how long it would take someone to do something if he smacked it right out of her hand.

"Don't you have someone to go argue with on Facebook?" Elias snapped, snatching his bag from the woman's grasp.

He couldn't help but wonder if his mother would have been proud that he'd had the good sense to walk away before he truly got angry. Her favorite thing to do was call him disrespectful. She would go on and on about how she hadn't raised him that way, but obviously, she did, because he ended up exactly that way.

Elias's mind was blank and his body stiff as he waited in the belowground pickup area. It wasn't long before his uncle pulled up in his black F-150, the same truck he'd had the last time Elias was in North Carolina.

"Hey, nephew," Uncle Mudiaga—known to everyone as Uncle Moodie—said as he got out and ran around to Elias's side of the truck.

"Hi . . ." Elias replied. The last time he'd been in North Carolina, he could have sworn that Moodie was at least fifty. But now, looking at his uncle—effortlessly throwing Elias's bag into the truck with one hand and likely able to do the same to Elias if he didn't watch himself—Elias supposed that every adult looked old when he was a kid.

Elias got into the truck next to Moodie, securing the belt around him. "Hey, Mood," he said as they drove off, wrapping his arms around himself and giving his biceps a reassuring squeeze, "I don't mean any disrespect, but I thought I was helping out in your store because you were reaching your golden years. How old *are* you?"

"I'm thirty-eight," Moodie replied with a laugh. "And I'm not too old to work. I just don't want to. I've spent all these years making money—isn't it time I go spend some of it? Let you young folk work a little bit while I go to Capri or Paris or something."

"We both know your ass isn't going to Europe. If you're still the same Mood I know, you couldn't leave that shop alone for more than a minute. You're better off just buying a baguette and some pasta right here and calling it a day."

"I see you haven't changed either. You've still got that mouth," Moodie said with a smile.

"It's good to see you, too, Mood."

That Uncle Moodie had started a business in his twenties was quite an accomplishment, but Elias would never say that to him out loud. Moodie would take that compliment to the grave with his chest puffed out and his chin held high.

"How's your mom?" Moodie asked.

"Good, I guess."

"How about Will and Nia?"

"They're good. Everybody good except me. I'm starving."

"We'll be home soon," Moodie replied, taking the hint that Elias didn't want to talk about his family.

They rode the rest of the way in silence.

"Hey, Eli." Moodie's voice woke Elias from a nap he didn't remember falling into. "We're here."

Elias stretched his arms and rolled his neck, earning him a satisfying *crack*. He then followed Moodie, half-dazed, up the stairs at the back of the bookstore, which led to the private entrance of the studio apartment over his uncle's store.

The bare walls, spare furniture, and layers upon layers of industrial white paint, which covered everything, including light switches and a few cockroaches, weighed heavily on Elias.

"This place is small as hell," Elias said. "I'd probably bump into myself by mistake."

Moodie brought in Elias's second suitcase and placed it in the center of the room. "It's either this or you live with me. I just thought you'd want a little independence."

"I'm not complaining, Mood. It reminds me of home," Elias replied honestly. He pushed his bags into the corner, where they'd stay, still packed, until he was ready to go back to New York. "Thanks."

"You're family," Moodie said. "Now, I'm about to go home. Do you want to come over for something to eat?"

Elias thought a moment. "Nah, it's cool. I'll figure something out."

Moodie put a hand on Elias's shoulder. "I know you don't want to be here, but I'm glad you came, nephew."

"Thanks. I guess I'll see you bright and early."

Elias dropped his belongings onto the floor and lay down on the bed, feeling the dull ache in his face as he shifted positions.

He rubbed his arm as he got up and walked into the small bathroom. He had to suck in and flatten himself to fit inside because the door hit the toilet, making it impossible to open all the way. He yanked the cord to the light bulb on the ceiling. It was more of a large closet than a room, and like most things in his life right now, it was just transitory. The mirror was distorted in the corners, and one side was a few millimeters lower than the other. He would fix it in the morning.

Elias leaned over the sink, his face centimeters from the mirror. The warped glass made his face bigger and gave it a cartoonish quality that terrified him. There were a few blue speckles underneath his eye, the whisper of a bruise, but thankfully, it wasn't enough to completely devastate his looks. He just appeared a little tired.

He pulled the cord to the light again and stood in darkness for a while, staring at his silhouette in the mirror.

"Tomorrow's going to suck," he muttered to himself.

KAI

The Day of the Concert
9:43 a.m.

Kai wished he could have gone to the airport to see Bobby off, but he was scheduled to work. He waited for a ride in the back seat of his parents' car.

The driver-side door opened with a *ding*, and Pop got in, clad in a Nike tracksuit and white tennis shoes. Mama emerged next, urging Pop, "Let's go. We're late," as she slid into the passenger side. As they drove off, Kai watched the sunlight flicker against his skin. He puffed his cheeks in and out until he was basically beatboxing, adding a rhythm to the barrage of uninvited thoughts he'd had since Bobby told him he'd be leaving—*your summer is going to suck, you're going to be all alone, that stupid candle isn't going to work*. He increased his volume to drown out the negativity, but Mama finally got annoyed and told him to stop. He was quiet for the rest of the ride.

"Careful with that boy today," Mama said as the car came to a stop in front of Moodie's. "I hear he's trouble." The uncharacteristic softness of her expression touched Kai.

"I'm sure he's fine," Kai replied, leaning forward to kiss her on the cheek. He gave his dad a gentle squeeze on the shoulder before stepping out of the car.

"Call us if anything—" Pop added before Kai slammed the door shut.

Kai entered the shop and waved at his parents until they were out of sight, leaving him staring at his own reflection in the window—a child with clunky headphones around his neck, scarred knees, and one of his shoelaces untied.

Figuring he ought to at least try to tie his *damn shoes* before Moodie came in, he sat cross-legged on the floor behind the counter and gave it his best try. His clumsy fingers knotted and jumbled the laces with every attempt. He looped and pulled, threaded and twisted, but his knots were either too loose and fell out or were too tight to accommodate proper circulation. He kept trying, nearly turning his shoelaces into a fire starter with all the friction. By the end of this, he would probably have no fingerprints.

The bell above the door suddenly jingled, and a voice called out, "Uncle Mudiaga, you here? How you going to leave the store empty with the door unlocked like that, Mood?"

A shock of embarrassment struck Kai in the chest. Hurriedly, he smoothed down his shirt and tucked his still-untied laces into his shoe. He prepared to stand, but when he looked up, the owner of the voice was already staring down at him from the other side of the counter. He was brown-skinned like Kai, with a similar build, but he was probably half a foot shorter, with broader shoulders.

Did he see me? Kai panicked.

"Hey, hel—hi. Sorry. *You're* Moodie's nephew Eli?" Kai asked, as more of an observation than a question.

"What tipped you off?" Elias replied, his tone shaded in dry humor. "And it's Elias."

"Sorry, *Elias*." Kai rubbed the back of his neck.

Elias seemed to consider Kai for a moment, then said, "You apologize too much."

It was an insult, but it wasn't in the cadence of an insult. It was more like Elias truly thought he was being helpful by pointing this out.

"I'm Kai," Kai said, extending a hand, which Elias didn't take.

"*Kai?* Mood told me your name was Dakarai," Elias said in an accusatory tone.

"It's a nickname," Kai replied. Using his once-outstretched hand to steady himself against the counter, he rose to his feet, causing Elias to take a subtle step backward as Kai's presence grew. With a slow and deliberate lean over the counter, Kai rested his elbows on its edge so he and Elias could be the same height.

Elias puffed out his chest. "How do you get Kai from Dakarai?"

"Ask all the people in this town who couldn't pronounce my name when I was a kid."

"Call-center name," Elias mused. "I get it."

The two locked eyes for a fleeting instant. A current of familiar energy hummed between them before Elias looked away and moved behind the counter as well. Kai's gaze remained fixed on Elias, captivated by the way he commanded the space. Elias reached for the forest-green apron Kai offered, and their hands brushed briefly. He felt a sudden weight on his back. Then a vibration pulsed through his body, and he saw a flash of bloodred. Without thinking, as if his hand suddenly belonged to someone else, he grabbed Elias's arm and held it.

The candle came immediately to Kai's mind.

Elias abruptly reclaimed his arm. "What are you doing?"

"I'm sorry," Kai said, mortified. "I—uh . . . the aprons can be hard to tie on your own. I thought you might need help," he said, fully aware that Moodie had tied his apron for him over a year ago and he'd been slipping it over his head ever since.

Elias gave Kai a sidelong glance. "Thanks . . . but I can manage on my own."

Kai's eyes followed each of Elias's movements, the way he confidently reached behind his back and how his fingers deftly manipulated the fabric. Elias pulled the strings tight and looped them in a knot without even having to look. Kai tried his best to appear casual, but the heat rising to his cheeks was hard to ignore. He was certain who this was.

Kai's pocket buzzed with a faint vibration, signaling an incoming call.

Bobby, you have such good timing, Kai thought.

He excused himself to the back room and took a seat on top of an unopened box of comics.

"Dude, I think something happened," he said as soon as Bobby answered the call.

"Why are you whispering?" Bobby asked, confused.

"Do you remember the day we kissed?" Kai asked in a hushed tone. He looked around nervously to make sure no one was there.

"You mean the day our love story began?"

"No, I mean the day it ended." Kai clutched the phone tighter. "Do you remember that boy I met earlier that day, the one from the park?"

"The one who sent you running into my arms? Of course."

"Bobby Bae! Stop joking for a second. This is serious." He held the receiver close to his mouth, and, using his hand as a shield, he hissed, "He's Moodie's nephew!"

The line was quiet for a moment before Bobby said, "I don't get it. Why is that serious?"

Kai ran a hand over his hair. "Last night, I was a little down about you, Winter, and Emmy not being here this summer. I thought I would do a— You're not going to understand what I'm trying to say. Let me try again," Kai blurted, not even stopping to take a breath. To anyone else, this would have been an unintelligible stream of nonsense, but this was Bobby, someone with whom he could communicate using only a series of grunts and facial expressions. "What I'm trying to say," Kai continued, "is that I put it out to the universe that I want to find love, and—"

"Don't tell me he's your twin flame." Bobby was governed by science and math—hypotheses with demonstrable outcomes—and he had no patience for many of Kai's views on life and love. It was part of the reason they got along so well; they constantly challenged each other. But sometimes Bobby's skepticism came off as patronizing.

"It's real this time!" Kai played with one of the short braids by his ear. "There's something about him. His energy is so intense, and his aura is . . . it's like . . . it's such a dark shade of red. I'm purple, so my head is always in the clouds, but he is so grounded. Can you imagine if an etheric cord existed between two people like that?"

"Kai, do you know how many times you've told me you've met your soulmate? You said this about Emmy last year."

"Then I found out her Venus is in Gemini. I could have ignored that, but our signs in the seventh house are incompatible."

"How about the girl you saw at the record store, or the one who checked you out at the movies last week? Or Jules from math class. Or how about—I don't know—me?"

"I know I try really hard to look for things that aren't there sometimes," Kai said, settling back and switching the phone to his other ear, "but this time I have such a strong feeling about it. This can't be a coincidence."

Bobby huffed out a sigh. "It's pseudoscience."

"Can't you just have an open mind for once, Bae?"

"I'm trying, but you're giving me some serious *But, Daddy, I love him* energy. I don't want to see you get hurt. Again."

"I'm not calling you Daddy," Kai retorted. "And I'm not saying I love him; all I'm saying is that I'm going to invite him to the CYPHR concert with me. And didn't you spend the better part of last year stressing over Winter?"

"That's different," Bobby replied, his voice suddenly smaller.

"Why? Because it's *you*? Since when are you so judgmental?"

"Since you ditched me on the other side of the country!" Bobby exclaimed, and the two fell silent.

They didn't usually bicker like this. Because the two of them were both introverted, they were far too polite to fight. The worst disagreement they'd ever had was back in seventh grade when Bobby borrowed one of Kai's graphite drawing pencils without permission and used it all day as a standard pencil—the tip was dull by the time he returned it. "Thanks for letting me borrow this. You're a lifesaver," Bobby had offered. But when Kai saw the blunted nib, his response faltered. "It's . . . cool," he'd managed. To date, that tiny pause was the biggest fight they'd ever had.

"I'm sorry," Kai said finally.

Bobby reined in his volume. "Me too. I just miss you already."

"I know." Kai buried his head in his hands. "I can't believe you're leaving."

"I can't believe you're *staying*. I'm going to miss the hell out of you," Bobby said, his voice breaking. Bobby was known to be a prolific crier.

And Kai was known to be a prolific empath. "Dude, if you start crying, I'm going to cry."

"You know I can't help it." Bobby sniffed hard and cleared his throat, pausing. "My flight hasn't even taken off yet and it already feels like you're trying to replace me."

Kai clicked his tongue against his teeth. "You know I can't replace you. I'm sorry I couldn't come see you off."

"I know you had to work."

"You fly safe, you hear? I love you. I'll be waiting for you when you get back."

"You always know where to find me. I'll never leave you behind, I promise."

"Don't do that to me, man. Come on!" Kai said, tilting his head back so tears didn't fall.

"I just called to say bye before Winter and I take off. I have to get to our gate. Just be careful, okay? I don't want you to get hurt," Bobby said, and then he was gone with a click.

Kai leaned his head against the wall, inhaling deeply to calm himself. A tear leaked from the corner of his eye and rolled down his cheek.

ELIAS

10:21 a.m.

Dakarai had barely said hello before he ran off. All alone in the bookstore, it dawned on Elias that the job probably wasn't going to be as easy as he'd anticipated. He had worked in retail before, but it was a shoe store, and he'd just had to ring people up because most of the customers already knew what they were buying. He stared at the many shelves of comic books, cases of desserts and pastries, and the complicated-looking coffee machine. He was out of his depth.

His steps were light on the creaky floorboards as he explored the store. It smelled like the chemical scent of ink, aged paper, and cardboard mixed with Uncle Moodie's famous peanut butter pie. Elias remembered running up and down the aisles with William when they were kids, before Nia was born. The shelves seemed so high back then, but now they barely came up to his chest. He and William would steal cookies from the case and get the books sticky. They would always hide the evidence, but there was no way Moodie didn't know.

Elias finally decided that Dakarai was taking too long. He was sure he could interrupt Dakarai's phone call for at least a second to ask how the speaker system worked.

He walked toward the back room door but stopped suddenly when he heard a quick, exaggerated inhalation followed by a few short sniffles. Elias rolled his eyes, muttering under his breath, "Is he crying? Dude is big as hell. How do his tears even know where to go?"

Elias peered around the doorjamb to sneak a glance. Dakarai's body couldn't have been more folded up. He must have been used to trying to make himself look small so he didn't intimidate anyone with his height. As Dakarai adjusted his position on the box, he grew like a shadow lengthening in the sun. He was tall and lanky, with limbs like branches. He had a small head with little braids, and a big crystal hanging from his neck. His T-shirt was just a little bit too small, and one of his shoes was untied. Elias clenched his fists, fighting the urge to stoop down and tie the laces for him.

He's really going to sit here and cry, Elias thought. *Everybody wants to cry. I want to cry. You don't see me boo-hooing.*

Eventually, Elias couldn't take it anymore. He dug around in the side pocket of his backpack and pulled out a pack of tissues. "Here," he said, extending it toward Dakarai, his head turned purposefully toward the front of the store so as not to make eye contact. There were few things he hated more than seeing someone cry.

"Thanks," Dakarai said softly, dabbing his face with one of the tissues. "I swear I'm not usually like this."

"You really don't have to explain yourself," Elias said, clenching his jaw.

"Sorry."

"Again with the apologies?"

Dakarai pulled himself to his feet, and Elias was momentarily surprised by his height once more. It only made him tense his jaw further.

"Did you need something?" Dakarai asked.

"Never mind, I'll manage," Elias replied, feeling a mix of emotions he couldn't quite place. "Take as much time as you need."

The door jingled with Uncle Moodie's arrival the moment Elias returned to the front of the store.

"Morning, Eli," Uncle Moodie greeted. "How'd you sleep?"

"I slept fine," he lied.

"Where's Kai?" Moodie asked, a hint of worry in his voice.

He took a step toward the storage room, but Elias blocked him. "He needs a moment."

Moodie's expression remained serious. "Why? Are you two getting along?"

Elias rolled his eyes, unable to hide his annoyance. "Of course we're getting along. What do you think I did to him? It's only been, like, twenty minutes."

Moodie circled the counter and used a knuckle to lift Elias's chin, his attention focused on the light bruising under his nephew's eye. Elias instinctively pulled away.

"I'll stay until Kai comes back," Moodie said. "I want to see him."

"He just had to take a phone call," Elias said, his stance stiffening. "Whatever he was upset about has got nothing to do with me."

Moodie raised his hands, palms out. "I'm not accusing you of anything. I just look out for him is all. He and his folks are good people."

"And what about me? I'm not good people? I'm *your* people."

"That's not what I'm trying to say—what I'm trying to say is that he's not like you."

Elias let out an incredulous laugh. "Why don't you tell me about myself, then, because clearly, I must not know?"

Somehow, he thought his uncle would give him the benefit of

the doubt, but he was doing what everyone else always did.

"I'll go, but why don't you come over for dinner later? We're going to talk." Moodie clapped a hand on Elias's shoulder.

He rejected Moodie's touch with a rough shrug. "Do I have a choice?"

"No," Moodie replied, and then turned to leave.

Elias folded his arms defiantly over his chest. "Who does he think he is?" he muttered under his breath when Moodie was already halfway across the street. *"Are you two getting along?"* he said in a mocking tone. "If Moodie wants us to get along, then fine, we'll get along."

Elias eyed Moodie's truck until it rounded the corner.

KAI

10:33 a.m.

Kai prepared to take the walk of shame back to the front of the store. He contemplated buying a plane ticket to the farthest country he could afford and starting a new life, but he knew he'd have to face Elias eventually.

Feigning nonchalance, Kai's stride ended up seeming awkward instead of apathetic. He expected Elias to make fun of him or, at the very least, give him a dirty look, but he was surprised when all Elias said was "For a second, I didn't think you were coming back. I thought you left me here high and dry."

Swiftly overcoming his surprise, Kai said, "High, sure. But dry? Never that." He forced an airy laugh and cleared his throat. "Are you familiar with comics at all?"

"Unless it was made into a movie, I've probably never heard of it," Elias replied, dismissively at first, but then his eyes widened, and he leaned forward. "What I meant to say is that I'd like to know more about comics. Maybe you could show me." His gaze traveled slowly down Kai's body, lingering at apparent points of interest, only returning to Kai's eyes when Kai let out a nervous laugh.

"Why are you . . . ?" Kai began, but then thought better of himself. "No offense, but I didn't expect you to be so nice."

Elias's expression darkened. "What did you expect?"

"No, sorry—I mean, not sorry. It's just—you're really . . . um . . . nice."

"Thanks, I think?"

Kai hoped that they truly were twin flames and that their etheric cord was strong enough to pull him from the hell of this painful conversation. He fidgeted with the captive ring in his ear in an attempt to hide his face. "I'll have you primarily work in the café, then, since you're not familiar with comics."

"What else will you *have* me do?" Elias asked, an unreadable expression on his face.

"Uh . . . I'm not sure yet. We'll see how it goes."

"Not used to being the boss, are you?"

"I'm not your boss."

"Not with that attitude, you're not."

Is he flirting with me? Kai thought.

Elias's lips twitched, his dimples giving away the smile he was trying to hide. He then pivoted, resting his back against the counter to squarely face Kai. He did that thing that boys who know they're good-looking always do: pretend to stretch but flex their arms in the process. Elias doubled down by going for a scratch underneath his shirt, exposing his stomach.

"Um, excuse me for just a minute," Kai said before slipping into the staff room and settling down at the computer.

He opened up his SeatTix account to create a listing for his extra tickets to the CYPHR concert but paused before he clicked submit. Leaning as far as he could without falling off the aluminum stool, he craned his neck to peer through the open staff room door at Elias, who was wasting time on his phone. It had not one crack or scratch, unlike the phones of most of Kai's friends, whose fingertips had callused over because of their spiderwebbed screens. Elias seemed above that sort of thing.

Elias glanced up and caught Kai staring. He winked, then turned his attention back to his phone, a teasing smile on his face.

Looking back at the computer screen, Kai chose "2" from the drop-down menu and watched the pinwheel spin until the page informed him that his listing for two CYPHR tickets was pending review. He had told the universe he didn't want to be alone, especially at this concert, and it seemed she had answered.

He'd wait for the right time to ask Elias.

Elias suddenly poked his head into the room, using the doorframe as support. "Are you going to keep hiding from me all day? I'm starting to take it personally."

Kai clicked out of the window. "Sorry," he said, instantly regretting the word as it left his mouth.

Elias laughed softly and shook his head before retreating to the counter.

After getting off to a rocky start that morning, Kai leaned into his role as mentor, guiding Elias through the more tedious but necessary aspects of the store's operations. Kai felt a sense of accomplishment as Elias gradually took on more and more tasks throughout the day.

When there was a lull, Kai pulled out his sketchbook and took a seat by the staff room door, where he had a full view of the counter and the entire front of the store, but also some privacy. This way, Elias, who was reading the coffee-maker manual, couldn't see what, or who, he was drawing. Finding his HB pencil, he began to lock this moment in time the same as he'd done all those years ago. Yet, it displeased him how bold and permanent his first few strokes looked, so he quickly switched to a 4H, the lightest pencil he had.

The shop's old factory windows were thick and wavy in the center, and how the sun shone through the panes made halos in Kai's eyes and surrounded Elias in colorful prisms, which Kai tried to capture with gentle strokes.

The two stayed like that for a while until Elias expressed his boredom with a protracted yawn as he stretched his arms above his head. He then set aside the manual, finally deciding to test the coffee machine itself. He moved with purpose, and soon, the *clunk* of a weighty mug bearing Moodie's face was quickly followed by the aroma of freshly brewed breakfast blend. Elias struggled with the faulty door of the pastry case before selecting a sweet potato scone, then perched himself on the counter near Kai with casual ease. A contented expression settled on his face as he indulged in a bite. "Do you want to hang out after work? I don't know anyone else in this town other than Mood," he mused.

Kai hugged the sketchbook to his chest. "You want to hang out with me?" he replied, excitement rising as he felt his chance to ask about the concert. With a nervous laugh, he joked, "What if I just talked about NFTs the whole time, then tried to sell you my mixtape?"

Elias shrugged. "You seem like you'd have some bars."

"I—" Kai began, but the bell above the entrance jingled. He mentally shouted into the void, frustrated by the interruption.

Elias glanced at Kai, as if seeking approval to handle this customer alone. Kai gave his blessing with a slight nod, and Elias immediately leapt into action. Elias leaned forward, resting his elbows on the counter in anticipation of the customer. She strolled over to him, her fingers lightly tracing the edge of the counter as she approached.

"How can I help you?" Elias asked, adding a subtle lip bite to the end of his question.

"Hi," the girl said. Kai followed her gaze and found that it was directed straight at Elias's lips, though he didn't blame her. Elias's jaw tensed when he said certain words, exposing that perfect little dimple, and at the ends of his sentences, he wouldn't close his mouth right away, so his tongue lingered on his teeth as though he was giving his words a chance to go back in.

"I'm looking for a comic book as a gift for my little sister, and I know absolutely nothing," Kai heard the customer say as he walked to the back room to give them some space while he continued to sketch.

"And here I thought you came in just to talk to me," Elias said. "I'm Elias."

Shaking his head, Kai let out a short laugh.

"You're cute. I'm Bri," she replied with a warm smile. "So, can you help me?"

"You've come to the right place, but you've got the wrong guy," Elias teased. "I don't know anything either."

"Then why do you work here?" Bri whispered behind her hand.

"Nepotism," Elias replied, dropping his tone as well. "And to talk to girls."

Kai snorted. "Corny as hell," he muttered to himself as he set down his sketchbook and stepped out from the back room. As soon as he appeared, Bri's eyes traveled up his entire body. The look of pure betrayal on Elias's face made Kai burst out laughing.

"Are there any other cute boys who work here?" Bri asked, playfully trying to peer around Kai.

"Just us," Kai said, hiding his laugh behind his hand. "Come with me. I can help you."

"So, it's like that?" Elias said. "You're just going to love me and leave me?"

"Oh, it's definitely like that," Bri replied as Kai led her away to the stacks. Kai glanced back at Elias, giving him a triumphant eyebrow raise.

Elias pretended not to be watching, but every time Kai glanced over, their eyes met.

After some deliberation, Kai and Bri eventually settled on the criminally underrated Squirrel Girl. He expertly wrapped it and placed it carefully in a bag.

"Before you give me my receipt, can you write your number on it?" Bri asked.

Her delivery was so direct that Kai felt there was no other option but to comply. That, and the fact that Elias wasn't even trying to hide how offended he was. Kai laughed and scribbled his number down. "I'll see you later," he said, sliding it over.

As Bri left, she offered a friendly wave to Kai, her voice playfully singing, "Bye, Elias," as she stepped out the door. It shut slowly, and as it neared the frame, a vacuum effect pulled it closed with a final rattle of the bell.

"It's the height," Kai said, trying to reassure Elias as soon as the store was quiet again, but he knew it was coming off as gloating. "Gets them every time."

"My dimples usually have the same effect," Elias said, seemingly dumbfounded. He stood up. "And I'm tall too. I'm six foot," he said indignantly. "In the morning," he added as he rose to his tiptoes.

"How tall are you in the afternoon? Like, right now, for instance."

"Give me a few minutes to do some stretches, and I'm pretty sure I could clear five eleven and a half, easy."

"*You're cute*," Kai said with a smirk, echoing Bri's tone.

The grin that stretched across Elias's face was a cultural reset. He seemed to want the tension to linger a moment before he asked, "Why'd you give that girl your number?"

Kai recognized this line of questioning. He smiled inwardly. "Because she asked."

"*I* asked first, before we were interrupted," Elias said. "I still want you to tell me about those NFTs."

"You play entirely too much. Are you ever serious about anything?"

"All the time."

"Then why don't you get serious about work and go find something to do, and maybe I'll consider it." Kai turned his attention back to his sketchbook, using the box he had previously used as a crying perch as a chair. He kept his eyes down and held on to his breath until Elias finally scoffed and returned to work.

What am I doing? Kai thought. He had never done anything like that before—using people to make someone jealous. But something told him that Elias liked to play games, and Kai would be lying if he said it hadn't been fun.

Even though it went against Kai's normal pattern, he decided he'd see how the rest of the day went before asking Elias to go to the concert.

ELIAS

3:56 p.m.

Elias stood behind the counter, tasting his latest failed coffee creation, his attention remaining fixed on Dakarai, who continued sketching. Dakarai struck Elias as delicate and overly sensitive—Elias had, after all, caught him struggling to tie his shoelaces and crying within half an hour of meeting him—yet he proved far more formidable than Elias had anticipated. There was more to him than met the eye.

Whatever he's ignoring me for better be good, Elias thought.

Dakarai tilted his head, surveyed his work, and then kept going. Elias tried to get a better look, but Dakarai caught him every time he tried.

With the excess energy Elias had from drinking so much caffeine, he felt like he could run a marathon and then deroot a tree with his bare hands. He had to burn off the restless energy or he'd probably start bench-pressing customers soon. He directed his attention to the dessert case, which had nearly snapped off his finger earlier when he tried to set out a new batch of Wookiee cookies. He found a tool kit in the staff room and got to work fixing the misaligned track.

The sun was just leaving its highest point in the sky, bathing the street in gold. Layers of oranges and yellows intensified behind the shops, casting long shadows on the storefront window and, consequently, Dakarai.

Elias occasionally glanced over at Dakarai, their eyes meeting for brief moments before the two went back to pretending they hadn't been looking. Elias couldn't look at Dakarai without him immediately turning toward Elias, waiting for him to speak. Elias tried again just for good measure. Same thing.

Elias finally decided he didn't care if Dakarai saw him looking; he smoothly slid the dessert case closed, put the tools away, and marched right up to Dakarai. "How are you doing that?" he asked with an accusatory tone.

"What do you mean?" Dakarai replied in his low drawl.

"How do you always know when I'm looking at you?"

"Because I can feel it. But I think the better question is why do you keep looking at me? Do you need help with something?"

"No, I'm just curious what you're doing." His eyes traveled down Dakarai's form and settled on his still-untied sneaker. "And because your shoe being untied for this long is wild," he added. He crouched down, a playful gleam in his eyes as he reached for Dakarai's shoelaces.

Dakarai stood up and made an exaggerated sidestep to dodge the advance. "What are you doing?"

"You're a liability in my uncle's shop, and I'm just being the change I want to see in the world," he replied.

Dakarai took another big step to the right and said, "You're making fun of me."

"Why would I . . . ?" Elias began, then stopped as it dawned on him that Dakarai did not, in fact, know how to tie his shoes. He'd noticed Dakarai struggling with it when he first walked in that morning but hadn't thought much of it at the time. "I'm not making fun of you," Elias continued, gentler this time. "Just let me do it. It's been driving me crazy all day."

"If you do it for me, then how am I supposed to learn?"

Elias knelt down and deftly untied his own shoelace in one pull. "Do mine, then. I'll teach you."

Dakarai glanced between Elias and his shoe several times, as if trying to figure out if this was a con or not. He finally shrugged, seemingly deciding Elias was being genuine, and stooped low, taking a lace in each hand. "Now what?" he asked.

Elias couldn't help but grin. "This is nice. I was tired of you towering over me all day."

Disapproval showed on Dakarai's face as he clicked his teeth. "You *were* making fun of me."

"I'm sorry. I'll show you," Elias said, a flirtatious grin on his lips, "but can you look up at me while you do it?"

Dakarai sprang up and took a step toward Elias, looming over him. A challenging glint flashed through his eyes, and Elias couldn't help but laugh. Dakarai definitely had a hidden edge, and Elias found himself unable to stop trying to get to it.

"You're calling me short in every single language right now," Elias said, amused. Dakarai started twisting his earring again. His earlobe was bright red—from irritation or embarrassment, Elias didn't know, but it seemed he did that a lot when he was nervous. "Can I at least see what you've been working on all day?" Elias leaned over, trying to get a peek at Dakarai's sketchbook, but Dakarai pulled it to his chest and crossed his arms over it.

"Come on, what's the big deal? You're not drawing me, are you?" Elias joked. Yet, Dakarai's eyebrows shot up, and the look on his face was pure terror. An excited smile spread across Elias's face. "You *are* drawing me. Let me see."

"Stop," Dakarai protested, hugging his sketch tighter as Elias made a grab for it.

Undeterred, Elias lunged again, but Dakarai held it over his head as high as he could. Elias laughed to himself. Basketball was his sport of choice, and he had dunked on nets much higher than that. He made another attempt on the book, this time successful.

"It can't be that bad. Just let me take a quick little look," Elias bargained. His arms became steel barricades every time Dakarai reached around his body to grab the book.

Dakarai suddenly stopped trying, closing his eyes for a moment, and released a long breath. He extended his palm and said calmly, "Could you please give it back? I've already embarrassed myself in front of you enough times as it is."

"Why is it embarrassing? Is it because you were only pretending to be disinterested in me all day?"

"I wasn't— You're so irritating," Dakarai said, letting out a defeated laugh.

Elias made a run for it, cutting through the staff room to the back storage room before looping around through the comic aisles to the front of the store. He flipped through the book, trying to find the page, but Dakarai followed after him, and, in the ensuing struggle, they found themselves breathless, face-to-face, only inches apart. A thousand emotions passed over Dakarai's face as Elias's teasing smile faded. He stared into Dakarai's eyes until he couldn't help but drop his gaze to Dakarai's lips.

The bell rang over the door. It didn't immediately register to either of them what that meant. It wasn't until someone cleared their throat that the two leapt away from each other, Dakarai pretending to be particularly fascinated by a random shelf in the classic horror section, leaving Elias alone to face Moodie, who had walked in holding a stack of his famous peanut butter pies.

KAI

4:47 p.m.

Moodie's eyes darted between Kai and Elias, suspicion etched across his face. He shook his head and went to the staff room to place the pies in the freezer. When his back was turned, Kai and Elias shared a look. "Say something," Kai mouthed. A mischievous smirk played on Elias's lips, and he winked, which Moodie caught as he turned around.

"Kai, outside now," Moodie said sternly as he gestured to the front door. He then pointed at Elias. "I'll deal with you at dinner."

Kai followed Moodie out into the humidity of the waning day, shoulders slumped, his gaze fixed on the ground. He had never been in trouble with Moodie before.

Moodie let out a long sigh and looked wistfully at Elias through the store windows. "My nephew really is a little shit, isn't he?" He tightened a fist and then released it.

Kai nearly choked on a short laugh. "What?" he asked, in genuine shock.

A vein pulsed in Moodie's temple as he ground his teeth. "He knows how much you mean to me and probably thinks I'm playing favorites between you all, so he's trying to win you over just to piss me off."

Kai's lips parted, forming a silent *Oh*. The reason Elias had been trying to charm him all day and was so insistent about hanging out after work wasn't because of any cosmic connection; he just wanted to spite Moodie.

Moodie's stare hardened as he turned his attention back to Elias. He shook his head and said goodbye to Kai before he took off in his pickup.

Kai observed Elias for a moment through the store windows, and it struck him that he knew nothing about this kid except he was here because he had gotten in trouble. He didn't know what kind of trouble. If he fled the state, it could have been a full-on felony.

Kai walked back into the store, past Elias, and lifted one of the heavy trash bags, the plastic handles digging into his fingers as he hoisted it over his shoulder. Elias grabbed the other and followed Kai to the rear of the store, and they tossed both bags into the open mouth of the rusted dumpster.

Elias took a bucket hat from the side pocket of his bag and pulled it low over his eyes. He produced Kai's sketchbook, handed it to Kai, and said, "I'm sorry, by the way. I promise I didn't look."

Kai hugged his sketchbook. "Hey," he said, calling Elias's attention. He figured he'd allow Elias a chance to tell the truth. "Do you still want to hang out tonight?" Elias nodded. "I'm not saying I want to, but if we did hang out, what would we do?"

"The South is known for barbecue, right? Maybe you can show me your favorite barbecue spot."

"I'm a vegan."

Elias's face dropped. "Not to worry. What about a movie? What kind do you like? I'm sure there's something out."

"I really only watch romantic comedies."

The disappointment grew on Elias's face. "Well, we don't have to hang out tonight. Maybe on a day off? Do you play basketball?"

"Nah, I don't really do sports. I do go to the court sometimes to draw the sunset, though."

"I'm guessing you probably don't *watch* sports either?" Elias asked, to which Kai shook his head.

Kai couldn't believe he'd been ready to go all the way to Raleigh with someone with whom he clearly had nothing in common. The possibility that Elias didn't like CYPHR or perhaps didn't know who he was hadn't even occurred to Kai. The concert doors wouldn't open until about 6:00 p.m., and the concert wouldn't start until at least 7:00 p.m., so they wouldn't get home until minimum eleven or midnight. That would mean they would have spent more than twelve hours together. They were already about seven hours into it, and Kai still didn't know anything tangible about Elias. Normally, that wasn't necessary for Kai to fall head over heels, but perhaps this *was* different, for reasons Kai hadn't anticipated.

"Look," Kai said with a heavy sigh, "I know you were just trying to prove a point to Moodie. I'm not mad or anything, but I think we both know we don't really want to hang out." He opened his sketchbook and tore out the picture he'd been drawing of Elias and gave it to him. "Let's just be cool, all right?"

Elias's expression was soft and discerning. He nodded, the drawing in hand, and Kai walked off without another word.

ELIAS

5:04 p.m.

The warm air carried an owl's hoots, which was the only sound other than the crunch of gravel beneath Elias's feet as he walked up Moodie's driveway. Lightning bugs flickered against beds of wild maidenhair ferns, a precursor to the even brighter stars above.

"Door's open!" he heard Moodie call from inside.

Elias went in and sat quietly at the kitchen table. Moodie's eyes bored into him as they sat across from each other. Elias's hand moved softly over his chest in a soothing gesture. He then lowered his head even farther to hide his eyes as the fluorescent light in Moodie's kitchen beat down on him.

"You know better than to wear a hat in my house," Moodie said.

Elias hesitated briefly before removing his hat. He held it in his hands, absentmindedly folding and unfolding it while keeping his eyes fixed on the floor.

"Look at me," Moodie said with a gentle command to his voice.

Elias's eyes scanned the room before he had the courage to meet his uncle's gaze. Moodie wordlessly got up from the table and started rummaging through the kitchen cabinets. He came back with a bottle of castor oil, emptied a few drops into his hands, and rubbed them together to warm the oil. He reached out to Elias, but Elias instinctively flinched.

"I'm not trying to do you any harm. This'll help with the bruising," Moodie assured him.

Elias tried to look anywhere but at Moodie as his uncle held his face in both hands and gently applied the oil underneath his eye with his thumb. Elias barely felt a thing.

"We're going to let that oil sit for a bit, then we'll clean it off," Moodie explained before he got up to start dinner.

The fact that Moodie hadn't immediately launched into his lecture was disconcerting. His parents barely waited for him to get inside the house before calling him everything but a child of God.

Elias looked around Moodie's house. His eyes settled on a collection of family photos on the living room wall. To his surprise, he spotted himself in one of them—a much younger version, around five years old, captured in a kindergarten portrait. He'd just lost one of his front teeth. And even though there was a gaping hole in his smile, he looked happy.

The smell of frying oil soon filled the house. Moodie stood over the stove, scooping up spoonfuls of batter and dropping them into the rippling oil of a black cast iron. He already had quite the stack of hush puppies on a plate laid with a grease-soaked paper towel.

"Looks good, Mood," Elias said, going to the refrigerator to grab a soda. He cracked it open and took a sip before settling back down at the round kitchen table.

"I know you're not just gonna come in here and eat my food without helping. Get up and set the table," Moodie said.

"Yes, sir, Uncle Mudiaga, sir."

It was quiet except for the popping of oil mixed with the clatter of the silverware. The air in the kitchen was uneasy, but Elias chalked it up to Moodie knowing he should say something to Elias but having no idea what.

"Hey," Moodie said as he sat. His neck was tensed as he motioned for Elias to do the same. "What did I walk in on earlier?"

Elias scoffed. "Does it matter? I'm an adult and you aren't my dad."

The legs of Moodie's chair scraped against the floor as he stood. "You're an adult. You can do whatever you want. But not when you're living under my roof. I've given you space and freedom, but clearly, you don't want it, so I'm going to give you some rules. If you break even one of them, I'm sending you home. You're right—I'm your uncle, not your father. I don't have to deal with this, especially when my business is involved." He moved to Elias's side and leaned over him, bracing himself against the table. Elias steeled his emotions, looking straight forward as if Moodie weren't there. "If you slack off at work, you go home. If you fight, you go home. If you disrespect my space, you go home. And Kai is your coworker. That's it. Do you understand?"

Elias's mask fell, and he found Moodie's eyes. "You can't be serious. You can't stop me from seeing someone."

"Maybe not, but I can give you a midnight curfew and forbid guests in the apartment."

This was that same noise he heard from everyone—his mother, his father, his sister, his principal, basically every friend or romantic interest he'd ever had. They didn't like his edges, but they didn't seem to complain when they could use them.

Elias folded his arms over his chest. "I really thought you'd be different," he said, his voice completely devoid of emotion. He glanced up to gauge Moodie's expression, but it didn't change.

"You've got no one but yourself to blame."

Elias bolted from the table and burst out of the storm door. It fluttered against the vinyl siding with a metallic twang before it returned to its place within the threshold.

He checked to see if Moodie was following him, but he wasn't. He waited around for a few moments, but his uncle didn't have kids of his own and probably didn't know that he was supposed to run after him.

A loud groan echoed from Elias's stomach. "Why am I so fucking hungry?" he growled. He threw his head back and let out a frustrated breath. "That's right—because I stormed out *before* I ate dinner." He kicked a rock and cursed when it scuffed his shoe. "I love hush puppies," he whined.

KAI

5:23 p.m.

"He *was* making fun of me," Kai muttered as he darted into the house, past his parents, and up to his room.

Elias never wanted to be friends; all he wanted to do was piss off Moodie. Well, he did, and he pissed off Kai too.

Kai took his frustration out on the air, beating his fists against it in a most uncoordinated fashion, when, finally, his anger converged on the candle he'd lit the day before. He had blown it out before going to bed last night, but something about it just being there was offensive. It was mocking him just like Elias was mocking him.

With a swift motion, he grabbed it from the nightstand and bounded back down the stairs, his parents' eyes following him as he charged through the living room and right outside into the backyard. In an instant, he had brought the candle down hard in the center of the cobblestone patio and was blasting it with the highest setting on the hose.

Mama forced open the window behind him, poking her head out and asking, "Baby, what are you doing?"

"Putting out a candle," he answered as he continued spraying the candle until it fell over and rolled away. He chased it with the hose, pushing it farther into the garden.

Mama's voice was kind and patient as she asked, "What happened?"

"A boy."

"Should I get the fire extinguisher?"

He considered it a moment before he shouted, "No, it's okay, Ma!" over the noise of the water stream.

Mama nodded and yanked the finicky window shut.

Kai charged through the living room once again and shut the door to his bedroom, muttering to himself, "I don't need Bobby or Winter or Emmy, or especially Elias, to have fun. I'll go to the concert alone."

Chasing the candle around the garden certainly made him feel better, but it didn't solve the pressing matter at hand: The concert was within two hours, and he still had two tickets. Hunched over his father's laptop, he posted one of the tickets for sale. It was a single seat, and not even on the floor, so it was unlikely to sell, but he was out a few hundred dollars from this failed venture and wanted to recoup as much of the funds as possible.

His finger hovered over the mouse as he impatiently refreshed the page every few seconds. He barely waited for it to reload before he pressed it again and again, his eyes doing rounds with the circle loading symbol. After several moments of this, a notification chime alerted Kai that the ticket to the sold-out show had indeed gone.

Another solo attendee, Kai thought. Perhaps they could be alone together. *Unless they bought their ticket specifically to be alone.*

He was overthinking it, as usual. Sometimes, for shows like these, people did go with their friends but ended up sitting in separate seats because they couldn't find two next to each other.

Putting away the laptop, he stood in front of his full-length mirror, trying on every single T-shirt he owned, only to discard them in a pile on the floor. He was left with one option—the last shirt hanging—because no son of his mother was about to wear a shirt off the floor. He sprayed himself with cologne, just as his father had taught him—wrists, inner elbows, behind the knees, jugular—which sounded more like a self-defense combination.

All that remained were his shoes, which he dangled from two fingers as he rejoined his parents at the dinner table, where they were having a date night. Hiking his leg up, he leaned his knee against the edge of the table so he could reach his laces and muttered, "I'll show him."

Kai's parents exchanged glances. "A boy," Mama mouthed, to which Pop responded with a silent "Oh."

Kai groaned as he once again yanked his index finger from the loop of shoestring he had made. "I don't understand how I keep tying my finger into the knot." As soon as he did this, the entire knot fell apart, and he had to start over.

"Dakarai Reginald Barbier." Pop's frustration became evident with the crash of silverware meeting the table. "Just do the damn bunny ears."

"Reggie," Mama said, admonishing Pop with his own name. "He needs to learn the proper way."

"Chioma." Pop's eyes were daring, but he quickly conceded, letting out an exasperated sigh.

"Maybe I should just stick to slip-ons and slides," Kai said.

"No," his parents said, their voices joining in agreement.

"You said you were going to learn, so *learn*," Mama said, cutting into her steak like it had done her wrong.

Kai's leg was starting to cramp, so he placed his foot back on the floor and massaged the tightening muscle in his thigh. Yet, he remained determined; he couldn't violate his parents' strict *no shoes in the house* policy just for nothing. He hiked up his other leg, positioning his foot on the chair and leaning his knee against the plastic-covered edge of the dining room table. He made a loop with one side of his lace and then wrapped it around the other side. His parents barely breathed as they looked on. It was time for the moment of truth. He yanked the shoestring tight. Victory was his. Though his finger was once again caught in the knot. His parents let out deep sighs and then turned their attention to their steaks, which were getting cold.

Kai decided to give the bunny ears method a shot. With careful fingers, he formed the first loop, then created the second ear, and then crossed them over each other. As he pulled the loops tight, a sense of accomplishment washed over him.

"Reggie, he did it," Mama said, smacking Pop with the back of her hand to get his attention. "I don't care how. It's about time."

"Take a picture, Chi," Pop replied, giving himself a pat-down. "Where the hell is my phone?"

"No time! I've got to get to the concert!" Kai exclaimed as he raced toward the door, feeling like a brand-new man.

"You sure you don't want us to drive you and your friends to Raleigh? Your father and I can walk around downtown until the concert is done," Mama asked as Kai paused to pat himself down— phone, wallet, keys.

He hadn't had the heart to tell his parents that his friends weren't going with him. They would worry too much or probably not let him go at all, and his mind was already made up.

"I'll be fine, Ma. I'll be back before the streetlights come on!"

"Very funny!" Pop called right before the door slammed closed.

ELIAS

5:23 p.m.

Alone in his new apartment and feeling restricted by Moodie's new rules, Elias replayed the day. He hadn't meant to use Dakarai to get back at Moodie; it just sort of happened that way. And it wasn't like all of it was disingenuous. He *did* want to be Dakarai's friend. Though there was no way they could be friends if they couldn't break bread together. *Could vegans even eat bread?*

Elias's gaze fell on his bag. He'd folded Dakarai's drawing and shoved it in there, unable to bring himself to look at it after making such a fuss. But he supposed he should. How could he face Dakarai at work the next day if he couldn't face a piece of paper?

Unzipping his backpack, Elias carefully pulled out Dakarai's drawing and opened it up. His mouth immediately dropped open. At first glance, it was like a black-and-white photograph. Each line was deliberate and precise, and the cross-hatching created so much depth, particularly in the eyes. Somehow, even in pencil, the drawing seemed to hold warmth and reflect light. The fact that Dakarai was able to see him this clearly made him feel exposed. Dakarai had pretended to be disinterested all day, but something like this couldn't lie.

Elias groaned and let the drawing flutter to the ground, but he already missed looking at it. Snatching the paper from the floor as quickly as it fell, he turned it in every direction, examining it at every angle. It was perfect, yet Elias couldn't help but think, *Where the fuck are my . . . ?*

His eyes slowly widened in realization. The line work and technique were much more defined and had obviously matured, but Elias recognized that art style immediately. He and William had taken Nia to the park near Moodie's house the last time he was in North Carolina. Elias had been watching his little sister while William was on his phone. When it was time to go home, he had to dispose of any evidence that he had allowed Nia to eat ice cream before dinner. The trash cans were overflowing, and when Elias tried to balance the wrappers on top, a couple of things rolled off the pile, including what looked to be a drawing. He had wondered why anyone would throw away something like that.

Elias had picked up the crumpled paper and unfolded it to find a sketch of himself. He turned in a circle, searching for the artist, but the park was empty. Elias glanced back at the bench where he had been sitting, realizing it was the perfect vantage point for whoever had drawn him.

He had wondered the same thing back then at the park as he did right now in Moodie's apartment: "Where are my dimples?"

He closed his eyes, and an afterimage of that picture appeared in his mind. Elias had always possessed a photographic memory, so the image was as clear as the day he'd first seen it. When he opened his eyes again, it was as if the past had superimposed itself onto the present, and he became certain that the same hand had drawn both portraits.

The paper was weighty and rough against Elias's skin. He

absentmindedly moved it between his fingertips, cursing aloud when he ripped a corner of it. He had never learned to be gentle. His finger slid into the tear, widening it.

Whatever, he thought. *I've never needed anyone before, and I don't need anyone now.*

Frustration surged through Elias. Before he realized what he was doing, he angrily tore the drawing in half. He crushed it into a ball and threw it into a corner of the barren room.

"Why did I have so much caffeine today?" He felt like he could hear his hair growing. He had energy to burn, yet there was absolutely nothing to do in this quiet little town, and he didn't know anyone.

"Fuck a curfew," he grumbled to himself after a short while. "I'm getting out of here."

Elias wandered into the night using only his memory of the last time he had been in town—up two blocks, right at the last sweetgum tree, then another three blocks until he reached a rusted bench, behind which was the bus station.

Hm, maybe I should check on Nia, he thought.

"What do you want?" Nia asked, not bothering to move the phone so he could see her entire face. He was stuck looking up her nose while she continued playing video games.

"I don't want nothing from you, big head," he replied. "I'm going to a concert, and it's creepy as hell at this bus stop."

"You scared?"

"Mind your business," Elias retorted, puffing out his chest. "How are Mom and Dad?"

"Your mother is getting on my last nerve. She keeps crying, talking about 'my baby' this and 'my baby' that."

"Who is she talking about?"

"You!" Nia said, like it was supposed to be obvious. "You know good and well she doesn't call me or Will her baby. You're her favorite."

Elias expressed his disapproval with a tongue click. "If this is how she treats her favorite, how the hell does she treat you?"

"Better than you treat Will." Elias fell silent as Nia continued, "Why are you even asking about them? I thought you'd be having the time of your life out there."

Nia's voice was grating on his ears, but he didn't want it to stop, because the silence would be too loud. "I miss home," he breathed.

"You don't sound like you. You good?"

"I'm good. Just don't tell Mom and Dad we spoke, okay?" he said. "My bus is here, so get off my phone. Behave yourself."

"Who are you talking to? *You* behave. And talk to Will. He misses you. We all do."

"I'll . . . think about it. Love you."

"Love you too," Nia replied.

Elias hung up. He clenched and unclenched his fists.

In line with his bus ticket, Elias waited impatiently for it to be scanned on his phone, then he boarded the mostly empty bus. It shook violently as it sat idle, its engine churning like a growling stomach awaiting its fill of passengers. He went all the way to the rear and stretched out in one of the rows, leaning his head against the window and propping his feet up on the seats next to him. He pulled his black bucket hat down over his eyes and then put his AirPods in.

♪ If we kiss once, we can't take it back
But if we kiss this once, I can kiss you again
Let's make another mistake
The first mistake is already made ♪

Elias would be tired for work the next day. *Whatever. I'll just ditch tomorrow,* Elias thought. *Why do I even care?* If Moodie was going to judge him so harshly anyway, then he might as well fill the role of the villain.

With only about ten minutes left of the drive, Elias checked his email containing his ticket so he could enter the address into GPS. Seeing as he was already late for the concert, he didn't want to waste any more time. He only hoped that the opening act would run long. As he scrolled through the email, his eyes happened to fall on the bag policy.

CLEAR PLASTIC, VINYL, OR PVC BAGS NOT EXCEEDING 12" X 6" X 12" ARE ALLOWED.

Elias eyed his black leather messenger bag, which was decidedly not very clear. If it were, everyone would be able to see his Swiss Army knife key chain and his outside food and drink, two things that were also not permitted in the venue.

He rented a locker at the bus station. He took inventory of his bag before leaving it behind—keys, some snacks for his return trip, a book to pass the time, and a few other odds and ends. The only things he really needed for the concert were his wallet and phone.

On the way to the venue, people kept smiling at him. And it wasn't those polite tight-lipped smiles that people sometimes gave in New York when you accidentally made eye contact, but they were genuine smiles like they were actually happy or something. He would have to get used to that. He had never had so many people greet him in his life; he was starting to feel like Siri.

Approaching the sparkling retro building, he took a quick picture before handing over his phone to get his ticket scanned. He was already about an hour late, so security didn't hassle him too much. The lobby was empty except for a few stragglers who probably drank too much too quickly and were dashing to the bathroom. The bass of the concert boomed in Elias's chest as he reached his section on the loge level. When the usher drew back the thick red velvet curtain so that he could enter, the full force of the music hit him, and his eyes immediately widened as he realized he was going to have to cut through all this chaos to reach his seat. He looked to the usher for help, but they just gave a simple shrug that said, *You're on your own.*

Using his phone as a flashlight, he shined it on the floor to find his row. He tried to be mindful of people's feet and their belongings at first, but the number of dirty looks and shoves he got was starting to sour his mood. He barreled through, hoping that he could just get it over with and no one would retaliate against him later.

The numbers on the seats were no longer visible, but there was one open spot in the middle of the next row.

Once he reached the seat, he closed his eyes for a moment and took a deep breath. When he opened them again, the boy in the seat next to him was already looking at him.

Dakarai?

He racked his brain trying to make sense of the situation. He prepared to ask what the hell he was doing there, but a sudden bang startled him, and he stumbled over a purse on the ground. Dakarai reached out and grasped Elias around the elbow, stopping him from tumbling down the tiered rows of seats.

When he regained his footing, he quickly pushed Dakarai away, embarrassed. Aware that Dakarai still didn't recognize him, he took off his hat and turned toward the light. A spark of recognition immediately lit up Dakarai's features. All he said was "What the fuck?" before a sudden blackout enveloped the entire venue.

Elias was sure he screamed, and he was sure it was loud, yet his voice got lost in the instant panic of the thousands of other people filling the space. He squeezed his eyes shut tight, the familiar fear of darkness taking hold of him. He'd never felt as exposed as he did in that cold, echoing room. His eyes flew open again, and, for a split, frightful second, he forgot why he couldn't see and panicked, clinging to the nearest thing to him, which happened to be Dakarai.

He immediately pulled away, but he felt a tug on his arm, and he stumbled forward, inhaling sharply as he found himself resting against Dakarai's chest.

"Stop moving, or you'll trip again," Dakarai ordered, slightly annoyed, the bass of his voice ringing in Elias's ear. Elias flinched, startled by how close Dakarai's mouth was, goose bumps erupting all down his neck.

The room was so cold, but Dakarai's body was so warm. Elias tried to breathe normally, but his chest heaved, and he was sure his heart was beating out of control as he felt Dakarai curling his fingers into his back through his shirt, pulling him even closer.

Elias's body relaxed, and, at least for the moment, he wasn't afraid of the dark.

13

KAI

8:04 p.m.

The sudden shift to complete darkness was disorienting, and the intensity of the stage lights was still imprinted on Kai's retinas. He blinked hard. When the flashes finally faded, he became aware of just how tightly he'd been holding on to Elias. He loosened his grip slightly, but Elias didn't budge, and his own fear ebbed away as he wrapped his arms around Elias again. He strained his eyes in the darkness for any clue about what was happening, when suddenly, the greenish-hued emergency lighting came on, casting eerie shadows throughout the audience.

An emergency announcement blared through old, crackling speakers: *"Ladies and gentlemen, we are currently experiencing a temporary power outage. Unfortunately, tonight's event is canceled, and your admission will be refunded."* There was a long, collective groan. *"For your safety, we kindly ask you to follow the illuminated emergency exit signs and proceed to the nearest exit in an orderly fashion. Do not use elevators during this time. Once outside, move away from the building and follow instructions from staff for further guidance. Thank you for your understanding."*

Kai faced Elias, holding the seat armrests to make a barricade around him when people next to him started pushing past to exit the row and evacuate. *My enemies are winning today,* Kai thought to himself. His body became a buffer for Elias, their clothes shifting together as he absorbed the rush of the crowd. His shoulders and the backs of his heels took the brunt of it while Elias kept his head down.

When the row had mostly cleared, Elias finally looked up. Pressed against Kai's chest, Elias suddenly seemed embarrassed by their proximity. He tried to pull back, but his earring snagged on Kai's necklace, causing him to crash right back into him.

"Let go," Elias said through gritted teeth, trying to forcibly yank his earring free.

"Stop moving so I can untangle it," Kai hissed.

"You're taking too long!"

Kai slapped Elias's hand, and Elias looked shocked. "Just let me do it," Kai insisted, taking a deep fortifying breath before easily unhooking Elias from his amethyst.

Elias brushed himself off, likely an attempt to wipe off the awkwardness that hung around them, while Kai stepped back to give them both space. But with so little room, he nearly tumbled to the bottom of the stadium. The fall would have been a welcome escape. At least he wouldn't have Elias staring at him like he'd just touched down from another galaxy.

"What are you doing here?" Elias asked in an accusatory tone. His eyebrows drew together, wrinkling his forehead.

"Same as you, I suspect," Kai replied, crossing his arms over his chest, suddenly feeling exposed under Elias's gaze.

"Let's just go," Elias said, looking straight past Kai at the ushers who were waving their lightsaber-looking glow sticks, directing everyone toward the exits.

Kai watched the muscles in Elias's back moving beneath his shirt, noting how tense he seemed and how focused he was on keeping his shoulders as squared as possible.

Definitely didn't do his stretches, Kai thought. He snorted, earning a cutting glare from Elias.

Kai followed him toward the doors, down the stairs, and out the way they had come in. Hundreds of people stood outside—some with purple hair, accessories from wrist to elbow, piercings Kai had never seen before, and more than one person in black lipstick. They had all been there for the same purpose, and now their purpose had been taken from them. All they could do was stand on the street and stare at the venue, probably out of some false hope that the ushers would direct them back inside and the concert would go on like nothing ever happened.

But no. Police cars and fire trucks came barreling down the street, lighting it up purple as the red and blue spun together.

The faces in the crowd dropped one by one, including Elias's. Kai could feel his disappointment.

"Did you take a bus here?" Kai asked after a few minutes of uncomfortable silence.

"Yeah, you?" he replied. His eyebrows lifted, and his eyes were bright. It was unclear whether he wanted Kai to say yes or no, but he got his answer when Kai said yes and Elias's eyes immediately darkened again.

Kai had it in his mind that he would go alone, he would dance with his arms in the air alone, and then he would get on the bus alone, and then go home alone, and then go to sleep in his own bed—you guessed it—alone. He didn't invite Elias to the concert for a reason, and now as soon as Elias showed up, the entire venue died. Perhaps he was an omen of ill fortune.

Kai scoffed. He should have chased the candle around the backyard longer.

He contemplated saying goodbye and walking off, or even walking off *without* saying goodbye. It's not like he owed Elias anything. But what if they ended up on the same bus together anyway? It would be like when you're saying goodbye to a friend, and you know that you need to go on the same direction as them, but you can't because it would be too awkward, so you go the opposite way and take the strangest, most elaborate route back to your house just to avoid the fallout. It would be exactly that, except it would be a forty-five-minute drive inside of what was essentially an aluminum can on wheels. No escape. And then they would have to see each other almost every day for the rest of the summer, if not longer. This was an introvert's nightmare.

After carefully weighing all his options, Kai finally suggested, "Maybe we should walk to the bus station and go home?"

"This is some bullshit," Elias said, taking an incredulous look around, as if he was waiting for someone to jump out and tell them that they were being pranked. "It's all those light bulbs outside. This building was probably built during the Cleveland administration."

Kai folded his arms, amused. "Which one?"

"The first one."

"Are you deflecting because you're embarrassed?"

"Why would I be embarrassed?" Elias asked, looking at Kai like he'd suggested the most absurd thing he'd ever heard.

"Because you looked like you were about to throw hands when I saved you from rolling your ass off the balcony, but then you clung to me like a baby koala the second the lights went out."

Elias paused for a second before saying, "Let's just get out of here."

Admittedly, the moment touched him. Kai didn't have any siblings, and usually, he was the one everyone wanted to protect. "This is your first life," Bobby would tell him. Bobby would always be the one to drive him around, to say something if Kai's order came out wrong, to talk on the phone if they were ordering takeout. No one had ever sought out Kai for protection. It felt different. Good, even.

The walk back *to* the bus station felt infinitely longer than the walk *from* the bus station. The ground was uneasy beneath Kai's feet; he was intensely aware of every step that he took. He didn't want to walk next to Elias, but he really didn't want to walk behind him either. Or in front. There seemed to be no good choice that wouldn't inadvertently send the message to Elias that Kai was either threatened by him, trying to exert dominance, or still wanted to be friends. Therefore, the two danced around each other like ballerinas in a jewelry box throughout their entire walk.

The pervasive din of the city was much louder than Kai was used to. There were so many noises and sights and smells all at once. Frankly, it was overwhelming. Yet, Elias seemed right at home in the chaos and downright mournful to be leaving it behind.

The two finally approached the bus station. Where it had been bustling before, it was now completely abandoned. They were the only ones rushing back home after the canceled concert. Everyone else would probably try to make something out of the night. He knew that if he were with Bobby, Winter, and Emmy, they'd be exploring the city and eating absolutely anything and everything in sight.

The bus station smelled like mop water, and the lighting in there was so harsh that you could almost hear it. Elias took a sharp right toward the lockers but stopped short when he realized the door to access them was locked. He pulled on the handle again, only managing to wiggle the door in its frame.

"What the hell?" He groaned angrily.

Noticing a sign on the door, Kai put his hand on Elias's arm to stop him from ripping the door handle off. He pointed to the locker hours. A vein began to pulse out of Elias's forehead. "Why is the bus station open twenty-four hours, but the lockers are only open until eight p.m.? What kind of sense does that make?"

"The locker room opens at four a.m. Just come back tomorrow," Kai suggested. "I'll cover for you with Moodie. Or even if you tell him, I'm sure he'd understand."

"No, my house key is in there. There's no way I can get back into my apartment."

"Moodie has a spare."

"It'll be late by the time we get back. He gave me a curfew that I'm deliberately defying right now. I can't ask him for help." Elias huffed. "I should have read the stupid sign. I'm not used to these country-ass hours."

"Do you want to stay at my house, then?" Kai suggested.

Elias looked sideways at Kai. "Trust me, I'm not the kind of surprise guest that parents like." He turned his attention back to the locked door. "How much force do you think it would take to break it down?"

"Probably enough to land you in jail."

"That wouldn't be too smart, would it? Our job really isn't the kind you can do remotely."

"At least you'd have somewhere to stay tonight."

Elias let out a long breath. "I swear this is just my luck. I want to go home—*home* home. Moodie is on my shit, the electricity is acting up, this door is trying me, and I haven't eaten since that stupid scone this morning, so even my own stomach isn't loyal. I have yet to be shown a drop of this Southern hospitality everybody's always talking about," Elias raged. "Of course, this city block is powered by hamster wheels, but for some reason, this door is made out of reinforced fucking steel!"

Kai choked out a short laugh but quickly stifled it.

The way Elias spoke was entertaining; everything was so urgent, and he took every little thing so personally.

Elias rubbed his chest a few times. "What are you going to do?" he asked Kai, completely ignoring the fact that he'd just thrown a full-blown tantrum.

"I feel like I got to go back or my parents will make one of those T-shirts that has my face in the clouds," Kai replied. "What are *you* going to do?"

"I'm going to kill time until this place opens."

Kai was instantly conflicted. On one hand, Elias could most likely protect himself and make it back home in one piece on his own. Yet, Kai didn't feel right about leaving him there. He wasn't from the area, and Kai wouldn't even walk his friends home without waiting to watch them go inside. There was no way in hell he'd be able to get on a bus and travel forty-five minutes away from Elias and be able to sleep soundly that night.

He sighed; there was only one decision.

"I'll stay with you," Kai said, in a way that didn't invite argument. "We can split a hotel or something."

"Are you trying to get me alone?" Elias teased, his demeanor shifting into that charm that had almost tricked Kai. Almost. "Is that why you followed me here?"

"Followed *you*? Aren't you embarrassed saying stuff like that?"

"*You* should be embarrassed," Elias retorted, folding his arms over his chest. "How'd you even know I was going to be at the concert?"

Kai's chin jutted back in disbelief. "I got there almost a full hour before you did. What kind of logic is that? *You're* the one who bought *my* ticket. Did *you* follow *me* here?"

"Now, how was I supposed to know it was your ticket? And I didn't even get to see any of the concert, so I want my money back."

"That's your late ass's fault." Kai pointed a finger. "The concert was canceled for me, too, you know," he shot back. "And you're talking like I'm the one who told you not to eat all day. Or like I had something to do with the electricity. You weren't complaining when you were trying to jump into my arms."

Elias had a meme-able expression on his face. He squared his shoulders and lifted his chin. "I don't like the dark. Especially in a place that big. Hold it over my head if you must."

"I'm, like, a foot taller than you—I don't think I have a choice but to hold it over your head," he said, taking a step forward to close the gap between them. Kai bit his lip. After a thoughtful pause, he asked, "What will you do if I don't stay?"

Shifting uncomfortably on his feet, Elias replied, "Probably sit at the bus station and wait. You know I don't like the dark, especially alone. I need a big strong man to protect me."

Kai looked all around in an exaggerated manner. "Is the big strong man in the room with us? Because I know you're not talking about me."

"Of course I'm talking about you. Don't act like you didn't save my life back there."

"Why not? *You're* acting like I didn't. Did you even say thank you?"

Elias looked up at him, his gaze shifting from round and curious to playful and teasing, with a half-lidded allure—a transformation so seamless it should be studied. "Thanks."

Kai put distance between them, rubbing the back of his neck nervously. "Don't . . . don't look at me like that, okay?"

"Why?"

"You know why." Kai waited for Elias to respond with an apology, an explanation, anything. But when the only sound was their breathing, Kai let out a deep sigh. He threw his hands up in surrender and began to walk away. "Forget it. I'm going home. Good luck! I hope you make it to work tomorrow. If not, it's been nice knowing you."

"Wait," Elias said with a sudden desperation. "Stay."

Kai had never actually planned to leave, but the look on Elias's face made him feel guilty for even joking about it.

"Fine," he relented.

They looked at each other for a moment until Elias's warm brown eyes seemed to startle, their quick movements betraying a sudden awareness that he had ventured into vulnerable territory. He did an about-face and started marching away, his bucket hat pulled low over his eyes. "If you insist on staying, you're taking me to dinner, and you're paying for it," he said over his shoulder. "And if I see a piece of kale or anything made out of tofu on or around my plate, I'm calling Homeland Security."

ELIAS

8:24 p.m.

As they walked to The Dive, the barbecue restaurant Dakarai had selected, Elias tried to hold in a sneeze but easily lost the battle. A dull pain spread over his face.

"You good?" Dakarai asked.

"It's just allergies. The trees down here nut all over the place," Elias replied, glaring at the greenery around him, meticulously maintained and even shaped into pieces of art. He pressed his fingers to the bridge of his nose to relieve the pressure, to no avail.

Dakarai eyed him suspiciously, and Elias yanked his hat down to obscure his face.

The two rounded a corner, and there, against the graying night sky, was an odd sight—the silhouette of a large acorn. As they approached, the size of the steel-and-copper art piece, its cap green with patina, became apparent. The acorn stood out against the backdrop of the corporate plaza surrounded by sleek glass buildings.

"What in the *Ice Age* is this?" Elias asked, glad there was something to take the attention off him.

"In New York, you have a giant crystal ball. Here, we have this,"

Dakarai replied, motioning proudly to the ridiculous thing. "We drop it at midnight on New Year's."

"What does an acorn have to do with Raleigh?"

"What's a shiny ball got to do with New York?"

Elias shrugged, and the two fell into silence again.

When they reached the restaurant a few blocks down, Dakarai held open the door and motioned Elias through with a slight bow of his head. Perhaps it was all that sweet tea they drank down South, but Dakarai had a gentle way about him, with a heart so tender it practically fell off the bone. And since Dakarai had chosen the place, that would likely be the only thing falling off the bone. Especially because, out of guilt over his actions, or perhaps sheer curiosity, Elias let Dakarai order for him, a challenge Dakarai accepted with relish. When the server came, Dakarai pointed out items on the menu without speaking so Elias would be surprised when his meal showed up.

The two were seated across from each other at a table tucked away in a corner near the kitchen. Every time the doors swung open and flapped back and forth, carrying a rush of noise from people talking and plates clanking, Elias grimaced. He was uneasy as they waited for their meals. The small table forced him and Dakarai close despite their efforts to scoot back as far as possible without joining their neighbors for dinner. In between glances at himself in the silverware, his forward-facing camera, and the windows, Elias dabbed at his nose with a tissue. His allergies were, in fact, bothering him—that wasn't a lie—but it also felt like he'd been punched in the face all over again.

"I feel like our food is taking a long time," Elias complained when he noticed Dakarai looking at him.

"Just take a breath," Dakarai chided. "It's been, like, two minutes."

Elias folded his arms and pouted. Shifting in his seat, he tore his straw wrapper into tiny pieces. When he couldn't make them any smaller, he began reading the menu repeatedly, as if the contents would somehow change. Meanwhile, Dakarai stared out the window, his gaze tracking each passing car. Elias knew he should apologize or at least be better company, seeing as he'd asked Dakarai to stay with him, but he didn't know what to say. They'd spent the entire day together so far, but they'd yet to have a real conversation, and what little they had revealed to each other made it clear they had few things in common.

Elias cleared his throat and opened his mouth to speak, not entirely sure what would come out. "So, um, what are your hobbies?" he asked. He mentally slapped himself for asking the most boring question possible.

Dakarai kept his gaze fixed outside as he replied, "I don't really have any other than comics and art. I draw and paint."

"What kind of stuff do you draw . . . and paint?"

"Um . . . I make webcomics sometimes, and I like to do portraits, mostly, which you know . . ." Dakarai's voice trailed off as uncertainty filled his words. "Did you like the portrait I gave you?" he asked in a low tone.

Elias's ears became hot as he remembered the way he'd tried so desperately to snatch the portrait away from Dakarai earlier. "I loved it, but," he said, noting how nervous the *but* made Dakarai, "that isn't the first you've done of me, is it?"

Dakarai couldn't hide his shock. "I—" he began but stopped when the server came to fill their water glasses. Elias was sure Dakarai understood his meaning, yet he chose not to interrogate it further, even after the server had gone. This was confirmation enough that it was Dakarai's drawing he'd found in the trash five years ago.

"What made you draw me?" Elias pressed.

Dakarai rubbed the back of his neck as he often did. "It's kind of hard to explain," he said with a nervous laugh. "I draw everyone."

"Oh . . ."

Then Dakarai hastily added, "But only people I want to know better. Because people usually show you one face and hide another, and I try to capture the one that's underneath."

"Oh."

Elias considered asking Dakarai which face he'd seen—after all, he'd drawn it twice—but he was afraid of the answer. Art could be about creating something beautiful. Of course, it was also true that the things we hate or fear could be muses. Elias had to remind himself that Dakarai never actually delivered the first drawing. It had been trashed. Perhaps he didn't like what he'd seen.

Elias and Dakarai tried hard not to make eye contact, fearing that it'd signal the other to talk again. Elias finally caught sight of their server, who was walking in the direction of their table.

"Our food is coming," Elias said, thanking every god he could think of that they could at least eat so they wouldn't feel pressured to talk. However, his smile faded when his eyes fell on his "pulled pork" sandwich. He squinted skeptically at it. Then, pinching the bun between two fingers, he took the smallest bite he could and quickly put it down again, as if he were afraid it would bite him back.

"What do you think?" Dakarai asked. His expression was hopeful.

"Honestly?" Elias asked, to which Dakarai gave an urging nod. "It's dry as hell. I'm about to piss off the server so she'll come back and spit in it." He chewed animatedly as though on cud. "How is yours? Yours doesn't look as dry," he added as he poked at Dakarai's barbecue "ribs."

"Stay on your own plate," Dakarai protested, swatting away Elias's hand.

"Whatever happened to Southern hospitality?"

Dakarai's lip twitched, caught between exasperation and amusement, as he cut off a piece and lifted his fork to Elias's mouth.

"Yours is so much better!" Elias exclaimed as he covered his mouth to chew. "What's it made out of?"

"Seitan."

"*Satan?* Are you sure mine isn't Satan? Because mine has to be the work of the devil."

"Yours was pork."

"Plant-based pork?"

"No, literally pork. As in it was a pig and now it's pork."

With his mouth open in disbelief, Elias watched Dakarai as he flagged down the server and ordered another plate of ribs. Elias hadn't had someone order for him since he was a child. When he saw people do it for their dates in the movies, he thought it looked annoying, but he had to admit that he kind of liked it. Even though, by the time the order came, Elias had already eaten the rest of Dakarai's meal.

Elias let out a satisfied groan and eased himself back into his chair. Taking out his phone to pass the time while Dakarai finished up, Elias suddenly stopped.

"CYPHR posted something!" Elias said excitedly.

It was a Notes app screenshot of random letters in seemingly no pattern.

FJSUWIZNPOKEGDPDDECCTW

Dakarai and Elias looked over the message a moment, turning their heads sideways to analyze it from every angle. Miming a pen and paper using the tip of his finger and the palm of his hand, Elias tried a few configurations, but the letters didn't spell out anything that made sense; there were too many consonants.

"Do you know what this is?" Dakarai asked, perplexed.

"His name is CYPHR. I'm going to guess that it's a cipher."

"Well, did you figure it out?"

"I'm not Alan Turing," said Elias. "I saw the post the same time you did." He expanded the caption and read it aloud:

HEY DROPOUTS! 🎤

I hate to disappoint all the fans who came out to Raleigh, so I've got something in the works for you tonight—a SECRET SHOW. The band and I need some time to set things up, so I've partnered with my charity, The Kindness Project, to bring you a scavenger hunt to keep you busy while you wait.

<u>Here's how it works:</u>
1. Download The Kindness Project app.
2. Complete each random act and snap a photo as proof.
3. Upload your photos in the app and receive a clue with each upload.

Collect all the clues to decipher the code above. No two scavenger hunts will be exactly the same, but everyone will have the chance to access an exclusive unreleased song, which will be the key to revealing the location of the secret show (if you don't figure it out before). Only the first 100 people will be admitted. Let's spread kindness, support the arts, and have some fun. I'll see you tonight, Raleigh 🖤

#CYPHR   #TheKindnessProject   #LeadWithKindness
#SupportTheArts   #Raleigh

Elias had always wanted to do one of CYPHR's famous citywide scavenger hunts. He began feeling around for his wallet. "Let's pay and get out of here. We need to figure out where the show is before everyone el—" he began, but as he spoke, he noticed Dakarai's lack of response. Dakarai didn't make any effort to move. He simply folded his arms, his face remaining neutral.

Elias slowly settled back into his seat, his excitement having dissipated. "You don't want to go to the show?" he asked, confused. Then he understood. "You do. You just don't want to go with me." His inner gentleman took over, and he put his credit card on the table despite insisting earlier that Dakarai be the one to pay. He then leaned back, crossing his arms as well.

"That's not it," Dakarai assured him. "I meant it earlier when I said I wasn't upset with you. It's me that I'm upset with for falling for it. I always seem to . . . fall for it. But it's a habit I'm trying to break." He quickly looked down to conceal an embarrassed smile. "We'll be working together, and things got a little weird today, but I think we're at a point where we can turn back and forget anything happened."

Elias's stomach lurched with guilt. This was exactly the sort of person he shouldn't have led on. That had been obvious when he found Dakarai crying, yet Elias had done it anyway. He opened his mouth to say something but couldn't think of what, and the two fell quiet for a moment.

The server came to take Elias's credit card, and while they waited for her to return, Dakarai busied himself with his phone. Elias had no idea what Dakarai could be doing on that ancient thing—perhaps texting in Morse code.

"Sorry," he said. "My best friend just landed in California. He's checking in."

The best friend again, huh? Elias thought.

They must have been close if they talked this much. Nia was Elias's best friend, but he couldn't say that he talked to her by phone once a day, much less twice.

Dakarai had a peculiar way of texting with his left index finger and right thumb, and he silently mouthed every word as he typed it. Each time Elias stared, Dakarai's eyes met his, causing Elias to quickly look away.

"I still can't figure out how you do that. It's wild," Elias said, rubbing his chest. If he could feel eyes on him, he would have seen Dakarai at the park all those years ago. "How does it feel when people are looking at you?"

"Don't act like you don't know what it feels like to be stared at."

Elias drew closer, resting his elbows on the table. "Who stares at me?"

"I don't know. People," Dakarai replied, gesturing around indiscriminately.

"Do you?"

The pupils of Dakarai's eyes quivered slightly before he cleared his throat and said, "I mean, you're attractive in a certain light," and paused before he added, "a really dim one."

Elias gripped the edge of the table and leaned in. "Why did you draw me, then? Tell me the truth this time."

He would have assumed it was the dimples—those were what everyone always noticed about him—but Dakarai had inexplicably left them out of the sketch.

"I don't know. I just did," Dakarai replied.

Elias regarded Dakarai with curiosity. "And what about the first time? That day in the park five years ago."

"How did you . . . ? I, um." Dakarai looked up at the ceiling, spinning his earring around before he said, "The way you were with that little girl was—I don't know. You were just so gentle with her, and you seemed kind."

"*Gentle? Kind?*" Elias repeated with a disbelieving laugh. "No one would agree with you."

"Maybe you don't properly show people who you are."

He really sees the best in others, doesn't he? Elias thought. If it wasn't so endearing, it'd be annoying as hell. Dakarai had to have been at least six and half feet tall with a name that got the squiggly red line treatment on Microsoft Word, and yet he made no attempts to blend in. There was no way the world was any kinder to him than it was to Elias, so how did Elias end up like this and Dakarai end up like *that*?

"Everyone's already made their minds up about me," Elias said, fidgeting with the hem of his shirt.

Dakarai's stare bored into him. "That's not true. *You're* the one who tried to make up my mind for me."

The server returned with Elias's credit card, and the conversation paused until she left again.

"Look," Elias said, stretching his arms above his head. "You're right. I'm not the person I was all day today at work. At least I hope I'm not. Just get to know me tonight, and if you still hate me, then we can just be coworkers, no hard feelings. But maybe," he continued, releasing a deep breath, "if you decide differently, we could be friends? You said you only draw people you want to know better. Well, here's your chance. I've got a phone from this century that can download apps; you've got knowledge of this city. Let's start over—clean slate—and do the scavenger hunt together. I want to know you better too."

Dakarai tightened his already-folded arms. "You do?"

Elias nodded.

"It would make this summer so much easier if we could be friends," Dakarai said, seemingly thinking aloud. "But you have to promise no more flirting with me."

"*Flirting?* Me? What kind of girl do you think I am?" Elias's mouth split into a smile.

"No smiling either," Dakarai warned. "If I see even one of your dimples, I'm getting on the bus and going home without you."

Elias saluted Dakarai. "Yes, sir."

He gestured broadly, his tacit way of telling Dakarai to lead the way. He quickly signed the check and slid it to the edge of the table before grabbing his things. Opening the app as he followed Dakarai out of the restaurant, he was prompted by a screen that said *Do not click until you're ready to begin the scavenger hunt. You will only have five minutes to complete the first action.*

He looked for approval from Dakarai, who merely shrugged.

With unsteady hands, Elias clicked the start button. A timer instantly appeared in the top right corner, along with an envelope icon in the center of the screen. The descending timer struck panic into him, like he'd slept past an alarm or was late for school. He swallowed his anxiety as best he could and clicked the envelope.

✉️

Random Act of Love

Hug someone for 10 seconds.

"Yeah, no," Dakarai said flatly, turning on his heel. "I'm out of here."

A smile spread across Elias's face—he knew he liked CYPHR for a reason. "It's just a hug," he said, gently stopping Dakarai by grabbing his arm. He took a deliberate step in front of him, raising his eyes to meet Dakarai's.

Dakarai bit his lip, hesitating for a moment before releasing a breath. "If we're going to do this scavenger hunt together, all of that," he said, waving his hands over Elias, "is what we're not going to do. Don't look at me like that."

Elias's lips twitched into a sly smirk. "Where am I supposed to look, then?"

"At the floor or the back of your eyelids."

"Fine," Elias said, his eyes fluttering closed. His hands felt heavy and useless by his sides, his increasing heartbeat pulsing through his ears, slowly drowning out the din. "Is this what you want?" he asked.

"It's somehow worse."

Elias's eyes shot open at the cool touch of Dakarai's hand on his. He could see the hesitation on Dakarai's face, but also the curiosity—the slight change in breath and a flicker of his gaze to Elias's lips. Hesitantly, Dakarai gently pulled Elias forward by the hand and then wrapped his arms around him, holding him in an embrace that felt as if it might be their last.

Elias blinked hard, trying to make sense of the situation, when Dakarai's voice, close to his ear, asked softly, "Are you going to take the picture?"

Acting on pure muscle memory, Elias raised his phone and tapped the shutter button, easing farther into the embrace each second as he counted down from ten with the timer, their heartbeats a metronome.

The photo snapped and automatically uploaded into the app, revealing two new envelopes. Dakarai abruptly broke the contact, forcing Elias to plant his feet firmly to resist the innate pull he felt toward him, the desire to continue being held. But with a deep breath, he refocused, redirecting his attention to the first of the two envelopes. Inside was only the number *0*.

"The hell?" Elias muttered, puzzled. But he and Dakarai didn't have much time to dwell on its meaning; as soon as Elias clicked on the other envelope containing their next task, a timer immediately started.

> ✉
> ### Random Act of Mindfulness
> *Don't miss your chance*
> *At seeing the beauty of Raleigh*
> *Like you've never seen before*
> *Take a look at the stars*
> *Over the skyline of the city*
> *Naming me to get to the top*

With the clock now counting down from ten minutes, Dakarai's forehead wrinkled in concentration as he scanned the words. Elias, on the other hand, found his mind wandering, the urgency of the moment unable to cut through.

"The spacing is kind of odd, isn't it?" Dakarai asked, tapping his chin. "And there's no punctuation."

"CYPHR's got me, a straight B-minus student, doing homework for fun on a Friday night," Elias mused.

Dakarai glanced at Elias from the corner of his eye. "Focus."

Clearing his throat and rolling his shoulders, Elias examined the clue for a moment. Running his finger down the left side of the words, he noticed the first letter of each line. "Does 'Dalton' mean anything to you?"

Dakarai lit up. "The Dalton is a hotel maybe five minutes away where you can see the whole city from the rooftop," he said. "We'd have to walk fast, but we can probably make it within the ten minutes. Want to go?"

He *really* did.

KAI

9:18 p.m.

Kai's shins burned as he and Elias speed-walked through the warehouse district of the city, past the converted industrial buildings. They had stark, angular designs with square brick exteriors and tall windows. The streetlights cast an eerie light on the building facades, giving them a haunting quality. Despite their harsh appearance, however, a romantic radiance emanated from a number of the windows.

Keeping his eye on the clock, Kai led them through the square, Elias quietly in tow. The hotel was only a few blocks from the theater and the restaurant where they'd eaten. Finally, they arrived, panting, desperate to get into the air-conditioning.

Elias opened his mouth to speak as he passed Kai, but Kai quickly put up a finger to silence him. "Whatever joke you're going to make about me taking you to a hotel, just save it. It's not going to be funny, and I'm not going to laugh."

Surprised, Elias snorted. "Wow, you sure know how to make a girl feel special," he said in an exaggerated Southern accent.

"Are you mocking me?"

"Yes."

"Just get inside," Kai urged, shooing Elias along.

A small group resembling the same sort of dejected and aimless concertgoers that had been left outside the Heritage Playhouse earlier crowded around one of the check-in desks. After a brief exchange with the concierge, the group hurriedly headed toward the elevator as Elias and Kai approached the counter.

"CYPHR!" Elias barked at the concierge while Kai massaged his sore legs.

The concierge recoiled slightly. "Do you have a reservation?" he asked. Noticing their confusion, he cleared his throat and rephrased. "Under what name is your reservation?"

Kai turned to Elias. "We were supposed to name him to get to the top. Why didn't that work?"

"*Naming me to get to the top,*" Elias murmured to himself, over and over again like a mantra, until suddenly his eyes widened and shone with excitement. "What's CYPHR's real name?" he practically yelled.

"Christopher Duke Kenney?"

The employee gave a small smile, then handed Kai a key card and pointed to the same elevator where the last group had gone.

Clearly proud of himself, Elias skated past Kai with his chin held high. Kai followed Elias into the elevator and rolled his eyes, but there was no malice behind it. The corner of his lip twitched with amusement he was reluctant to fully show.

Elias rested against the stainless-steel wall of the elevator, his arms crossed indignantly over his chest. "Are you going to scan the card, or do you just want to stand here and stare at each other until our time runs down?" he asked, one of his smug little dimples poking out.

"Maybe I just wanted to be in the elevator with you," Kai said, mocking Elias's accent. He stretched across Elias to reach the elevator controls with the card. Number nine lit up, and the elevator jerked into motion. Kai held Elias's gaze as he leaned against the wall as well, their matched eagerness to get to the top filling the small space. There was only about a minute and thirty seconds to spare and no way to make the elevator go any faster.

Despite wanting to bolt from the elevator when it got to the ninth floor, Kai let Elias go first.

He watched as Elias fumbled through his phone looking for The Kindness Project app, then aimed his front-facing camera at the both of them, adjusting it to capture as much of the sky above them as possible as well. Kai went to put an arm around Elias's shoulder but thought better of it—it felt too familiar, too friendly. He reached for the waist instead, but that didn't feel right, either, so he ended up stuffing his free hand in his pocket. They both tilted their heads back, gazed upward, and *click*.

Relief instantly set in when they were greeted in the app by a small envelope icon that bounced before opening to reveal a single number: *1*.

"Hm, a zero and now a one. What does it mean?" Kai wondered aloud.

"Is it a point system?" Elias asked. "I didn't know we were getting graded on this."

"Maybe our picture wasn't good enough?" Kai suggested.

Kai was debating whether an arm on the shoulder or around the waist would've scored them more points when a second envelope, another random act of mindfulness, appeared with the simple instructions *Enjoy the view of the city* and a ten-minute timer.

Now, with a jumble of letters from the original post and the numbers *1* and *0*, Kai and Elias weren't any closer to figuring out

CYPHR's message. At first, Kai thought it must be some kind of word puzzle, like sudoku or a crossword. It seemed unlikely now, however.

He decided not to wrinkle his brain too much trying to figure it out until they got more clues. Elias agreed, and they decided to enjoy the view as CYPHR directed.

There was a pergola made of industrial metal beams with café lights strung between the rafters. The rest of the rooftop was mostly barren, concrete slabs running from edge to edge. The disparity between the rigid design and the soft summer breeze created a calming balance. Elias walked to the edge and leaned over the cable railing, inhaling deeply as he observed the view. Kai followed his gaze to a few of the buildings that were brightly lit with a radioactive green.

"Why do those buildings look like somewhere the Green Goblin would fly out of?" Elias joked as Kai joined him.

Kai draped his arms over the railing and let them hang freely as he looked out over the skyline. "So, you do know a little something about comics," he said, more of a statement than a question.

"If I do, does that mean I get a raise?"

"Can you name a publisher other than DC or Marvel?"

"Um . . . no?"

"Then no."

The two sat with their legs folded in front of the view from the parapet. Elias's skin glistened as it pulled all the purples and greens and blues from the city lights. They leaned back and had full view of not only the bright city lights but also the stars above. They were faint, but the formations were unmistakable if you knew where to look.

"So, why did you go to the concert by yourself? I hope you

don't mind me asking," Kai said after a few minutes of comfortable silence had passed.

Elias wet his lips with a flick of his tongue. "Still asking permission to talk to me?"

"Tell me why you went to the concert by yourself," Kai said, more sternly this time.

A satisfied grin spread across Elias's face. "I like CYPHR, and I didn't have anyone to go with. Moodie also gave me a curfew, and I knew it would piss him off."

He really is *a little shit,* Kai thought, remembering what Moodie had said.

"What about you?" Elias asked. "Why'd you go to the concert alone?"

Kai twisted his necklace around his finger as he spoke. "I had tickets for me and my friend, but he bailed last minute. Now it looks like I'm spending the summer by myself."

"What the hell am I, a ghost?"

Kai pursed his lips. "I've known you for less than a day. I've known Bobby for over a decade."

Elias raised an eyebrow. "You and this Bobby guy seem really close."

"I feel like you're suggesting something, and if you are, you're wrong. We're just friends."

"Are you sure?"

Kai glanced over to see Elias's reaction as he said, "We kissed once," but Elias remained stoic, so he conceded. "It was years ago, though, and it made sense at the time. We were playing video games and eating a bunch of junk, and he kissed me. Honestly, it was awful, and it tasted like Swedish Fish, and it never happened again."

Elias looked like he might say something for a second, but he just laughed instead. Then he pointed toward a cluster of stars, tracing a shape in the air as he connected the points. "That's my zodiac sign."

Kai incredulously followed Elias's gaze and nodded. "Libra, huh? Tell me more."

"Well," Elias began, "Libras are known for their beauty. We're also ruled by Uranus, the planet of humility." Emphatically pointing toward the sky, Elias explained, "My Moon is in Gemini and my rising sign is also in Gemini. That's why my face is so symmetrical and I'm twice as attractive. Gemini is ruled by twins, after all," he continued.

"So, your beauty is written in the stars?"

"You tell me."

"You're not even a Libra, are you?" Kai said dryly.

"I have no idea. I didn't think you'd let me talk for that long." Elias's expression became discerning. "What sign do you think I am?"

"Based on all that nonsense that just came out of your mouth, Pisces," Kai replied without hesitation. "When's your birthday?"

"March fifteenth."

The corners of Kai's mouth slowly drew into a smile. "I knew it."

A moment of genuine shock reflected on Elias's face. "How did you know?"

"The symbol for Pisces is two fish swimming in opposite directions, which represents the separation between reality and fantasy, meaning you're the king of illusion and delusion."

He immediately turned to observe Elias's reaction—amused affront—and smiled to himself, pleased.

Elias's eyes betrayed a pointed interest. "You really believe in this kind of stuff, huh?"

"Even if the formations don't tell us anything, isn't it cool to know exactly where the stars and planets were the moment we were born? It's weird to know they'll never be like that again. Who am I to think that something as big as the galaxy doesn't have an effect on something as small as me?"

"You're not that small."

"Shut up," Kai said, pushing Elias, who rebounded like a free-standing punching bag. "But to be honest, I don't know what I believe anymore. Bobby's been telling me for years that all the astrology, tarot cards, palm readings, and stuff I do are bullshit. He'd never let me do any readings for him because 'There's no scientific basis for it.' Maybe I'm starting to think he's right."

None of his readings had indicated that his friends would be leaving him that summer, and he'd been wrong about the instant connection he thought he'd felt with Elias as well. Looking back, most of the actions he'd taken in his life because of the stars or the universe had led him to heartbreak. Because he always looked up at things that were bigger than him, he didn't realize how narrow he'd allowed his thinking to become. The definition of *insanity* was doing the same thing over and over expecting different results, so perhaps all the times Bobby had called him crazy, he was right.

"No offense, but your friend Bobby seems like a dick," Elias said, knowing full well that his words would indeed cause offense. "Read *my* palm. I'll tell you what's true or not."

Kai studied him, taking in his restless energy, the way he seemed to constantly switch between a teasing half smile and a full-body frown. *Stop trying to psychoanalyze him,* Kai thought.

With a shrug, he asked, "Can I have your hand?"

"Like . . . in marriage? You really do fall fast," Elias joked, earning a deep sigh steeped in disappointment from Kai. "Relax.

I'm only kidding." He showed Kai his palms, revealing several calluses running parallel to his heart lines. "I'm not sure what you'll see, though. Except that I dunked a basketball a bit too hard a few times." He hesitated briefly before finally extending his left one.

His skin was rough against Kai's palm. There was a warmth that passed between them, that intense red energy that Kai had felt earlier.

ELIAS

9:26 p.m.

Elias quickly turned his hand over in Dakarai's when he remembered that the skin on his middle knuckle had unzipped, revealing reddened flesh. It was an injury from slicing sweet potatoes with a mandoline and not from the fight as Dakarai would probably assume. Dakarai's gentle touch on his palm carried a comforting chill.

Dakarai blinked hard a few times. "What I'm seeing immediately is that physically, you're strong, but emotionally, you're timid." Elias narrowed his eyes, not sure if Dakarai was using this reading as a way to make fun of him. "Don't worry. I won't tell anyone," Dakarai reassured him. He then cleared his throat and continued, tracing the grooves in Elias's hand with the tip of his finger. "You do a lot for people, sometimes without them even knowing. You probably have a habit of saying that you won't do it again, but not even that deep down, you know you will. You're focused and make decisions easily; you're realistic but not closed-minded. You're emotionally intelligent when it comes to other people's needs, but when it comes to yourself, you tend to be self-sacrificing."

Elias looked at Dakarai sideways. "You got all that from my palm?"

Dakarai winked and gestured for Elias's other hand. He ran his fingers over each crevice, moving it to catch the shadows in every line and crease. "You want something, but you don't know what it is. You want answers, but you don't know the questions."

Elias watched Dakarai's mouth as he spoke. *Is he for real with all this clairvoyance stuff?*

"And what about my life line? Are you going to tell me I'm going to die young like everyone else does?"

"No," Dakarai said resolutely. "You're going to live a very long life. Exceptionally long, according to your life line. Maybe to a hundred."

"*One hundred years?* That sounds miserable."

"Should I go on?" Dakarai asked with a smirk. "We can talk about your love line," he said, adding, "if you're brave enough."

Elias firmed his jaw and took a deep breath. "Do your worst."

Dakarai, picking up where he left off, said, "You don't fall in love easily, but when you do, you *really* do."

The smile fell right off Elias's face.

"What? You've never been in love? Or you don't believe in it?" Dakarai asked.

"Both, and how do I know you aren't basing this 'reading' on things you already know about me?"

"Because you are the most talkative closed book I've ever met. You distract people by talking a bunch of shit," Dakarai said. "They don't even realize you haven't revealed anything about yourself. I may as well have met you five minutes ago." He ran his fingers along Elias's hand one last time before closing it up and giving it back to him like a sacred offering. "The calluses on your hand make it hard to see where your heart line ends, and I can't see the lines on the side that would tell me how many serious relationships you'll have."

"My hand *would* be the one to tell me I'm going to be alone forever," Elias said with a grin. He let out a breath and then leaned back, propping himself up on his arms again. "Enough about me, already. What does *your* heart line say?"

Dakarai's hands were long and bony, with veins that ran up his arms like tree roots. The edges of his nails were stained black, presumably from paint or some other art supply that was resistant to washing—the true hands of an artist.

"Well, according to my palm, I'm a true romantic, because I've got one deep soulmate line." He showed Elias, pointing to the side of his hand below his pinkie. The line was as dark as if something had burned it into his skin. "But according to me, who knows?"

Elias examined his own hands. Dakarai was right: Either he didn't have any soulmate lines, or his hands were just too damaged to tell. "You don't believe in soulmates? You seem like you would."

"I don't know anymore."

"I think you only start believing in stuff like that after it happens to you anyway," Elias said, "like people who don't start believing in God until they have a near-death experience."

The two fell silent, both leaning against the rail, their backs to the city. Dakarai's dark eyes bored straight into Elias's, making his heart beat loudly in his ears.

"It's such a nice night," Dakarai said after a few moments of comfortable silence. He had one of those voices that could cause a hush over a room, which seemed to startle Dakarai every time he spoke. He always started his sentences louder than he finished them.

"Do you like how you talk?" Elias asked, catching Dakarai off guard.

"What?" Dakarai laughed. "You mean my voice?"

"Yeah, or just how you sound."

He was quiet a moment. "I've never really thought about it. Do you like how you talk?"

"Hell no," Elias retorted. "Every time I open my mouth, it's like my whole neighborhood comes out."

"You do say *talk* weird. *Tawk*."

"You *tawk* slow as hell. Everybody down here does."

"You got somewhere to be?"

Elias bit back a smile. "Yeah, and so do you. We have a scavenger hunt to get back to."

He showed Dakarai the phone, and they watched the timer hit zero before a new envelope icon appeared containing another number, *1*, and the next task.

✉

Random Act of Connection

Make a new friend.

KAI

9:33 p.m.

Looking around at the pockets of friends siloed in their own corners of the rooftop, Kai bristled at the thought of having to talk to them. "How are we going to make a friend in ten minutes? I couldn't tell you the last time I made a new friend," Kai conceded. "I don't even think I know how."

Elias's shoulders stiffened. "I repeat, what the hell am I, a ghost?"

"If you're so convinced that we're friends now, let's take a picture of us?"

"That's no fun," Elias responded. "And we took the first photo together. They probably won't accept it. Making friends is easy. Just go up to someone and be like, 'Hey, want to be friends?' And then boom, you're friends."

"Then why didn't you do that to get somebody to go to the concert with you?"

"Did you ever consider that maybe I wanted to go by myself?" he replied, bouncing his palm off Kai's forehead in a playful manner.

Kai peered around at the other scavenger hunters, running down their own ten-minute timers.

"Don't look at them. Look at me," Elias said, drawing Kai's

attention. "These people are competition. Let's get out of here."

Elias stuck closely to Kai as they exited the hotel, passing by the same concierge as before. The glow of streetlights and neon storefront signs shone all along the tree-lined stretch. The sounds of laughter and music swelled. Plumes of steam that smelled of smoky barbecue and sizzling meats wafted from the nearby food hall, bringing the viscous scent of thick cooking oil with it.

Kai stopped Elias by the arm. "We don't have that much time. Go test your theory. Go up to someone and ask them to be friends, and I'll believe it works when I see it."

"Challenge accepted," Elias declared. His head immediately swiveled, scanning their surroundings for unsuspecting prey. He smiled when his gaze locked on a boy sitting beneath a red bus stop shelter. He appeared to be around their age, if not a few years older.

Before Kai had a chance to call off the bet to save himself from secondhand embarrassment, Elias was already striding across the street. Kai observed through his fingers. There was no way this was going to work. He winced when he heard Elias say, "Hey! Do you want to be friends?"

He tried to imagine the same thing happening to him, some random person coming up to him on the street asking to be friends. He'd probably assume it was an abduction or someone trying to recruit him into a cult.

The boy, who had seemed bored and disinterested before, now wore a smile that illuminated his face with amusement and a hint of confusion as Elias attempted small talk. The conversation wasn't audible, but it was evident that Elias had succeeded when they posed for a photo together, then exchanged phones and switched back.

"Pretty privilege," Kai muttered to himself. Elias really was the king of delusion if he thought this would work for the rest of the world.

"All right, I'll see you later!" Elias called as he ran back to Kai. "I told you it was that easy." He was biting his lip to contain a triumphant smile. "His name is Joshua, he does MMA, he's originally from Pennsylvania, and he's on his way to work as a security officer. We're moots now," he explained as he showed Joshua's profile to Kai.

All Joshua's pictures were taken in the gym. He was either looking in the mirror with his headphones on and a towel around his neck, or he was flexing his muscles, once again in a mirror, with a towel around his neck. Sometimes he was outside, doing parkourtype moves all around the city, swinging on scaffolding and doing ab workouts on street signs while one of his friends hyped him up in the background. There was a picture of him holding up his wrist, which was cuffed in a hospital bracelet, like it was a Rolex. His eye was black and blue. The caption read OCCUPATIONAL HAZARD.

"You know, I kind of see the similarities between you guys now," Kai said in a goading voice. "Are you sure he didn't think you were asking him out?" He folded his arms purposefully over his chest.

"I feel like you're suggesting something, and if you are, you're wrong. We're just friends," Elias said, mocking Kai's words from earlier, earning him a cutting stare. "Anyway, I proved my theory, so now it's your turn." The mischief in his eyes matched his grin. "I'm giving you a side quest to complete at any point tonight. I dare you to make a new friend. Your best friend is going to make a ton of new friends out in California. You should too."

"Hm." Kai scratched his chin. "What do I win if I complete the dare?"

"Whatever you want," Elias replied with a shrug. "Within reason, of course."

Kai wanted to say *Hell no*, but what came out was "Deal."

The idea of him and Bobby making new friends had crossed Kai's mind once or twice, but now, with Bobby actually gone, it felt more real. Kai and Bobby would have new people in their lives, people the other didn't even know. Nothing had prepared Kai for this gnawing feeling of betrayal. He glanced at Elias. It had only been one day, and Kai was already spending time with someone new. With more time, it would only get worse.

He pushed the thought from his mind.

Elias had his neck craned over his phone, a discerning look on his face. He had uploaded his photo with Joshua and received a new envelope. The two watched the app circle until a new number, *2*, and a new task were revealed:

Random Act of Mindfulness

Head to the Art District for your next clue,
Where two things you cannot escape wait for you.
On the path with one start, you must wend—
Choose wisely your way to reach the end.

"What are two things you can't escape?" Elias asked, squinting as he read the clue again and again.

"Death is probably one of them," Kai suggested.

Elias suddenly grabbed Kai's arm and exclaimed, "Ben Franklin!" His grip tightened as he added, "Taxes!"

"Wait—Death & Taxes is a restaurant," Kai realized. "We have ten minutes. Let's go!"

ELIAS

9:49 p.m.

Before Elias and Dakarai could get to the restaurant, they had to maneuver through crowds headed to a concert at the large outdoor amphitheater Red Hat. A DJ was in the middle of a pre-show hype-up, and the music boomed through the streets. Elias and Dakarai quickly walked by couples holding hands, groups of friends laughing, and overturned e-scooters in the grass. Despite the activity, there was a stillness and calm to the city that Elias enjoyed. Most of the stores had up their neon CLOSED signs. The rumble of passing cars felt meditative, and he would catch little bites of conversation from passersby. Elias had a hard time ignoring the romantic charm.

When they arrived at Death & Taxes, Dakarai took Elias's arm and brought him around to the back of the restaurant, where there was a large mural depicting a maze made of fire escapes. The mural started with a painted window at the top, followed by an intricate network of fire escapes that culminated in a single ladder at the bottom, leading to the ground. They had to navigate from the painted window of the mural to the real parking lot below, all within their remaining three minutes.

Dakarai traced the air with one finger, like he was making a painting in the sky. Elias watched him, his cool demeanor still unshaken and a low hum coming from deep within his throat though the time was dwindling. Dakarai wore the same expression he did as when he drew Elias, completely focused, only furrowing his brow or twitching his lip when he hit dead ends. The painting wasn't coming together quickly enough, and he dropped his arm in frustration, looking to Elias for rescue.

Elias closed his eyes, rubbing his temples as he visualized the mural in his mind, mentally climbing up and down the metal steps and ladders, searching for a way to the bottom.

"Got it," Elias said after a moment. He stepped behind Dakarai, gently sliding his hand over his. "May I?" he asked, and Dakarai nodded. Elias then guided Dakarai's finger through the air, tracing the correct path—up and down, left and right—until they both reached the bottom of the maze together.

"Your mind is so rare," Dakarai said, his sincerity making Elias's face flush with heat.

"*Tch*, whatever," he replied, playfully pushing Dakarai away.

They huddled over Elias's phone, their shoulders brushing as the light illuminated their faces. With steady hands, Dakarai traced the correct path through the maze, solving it and submitting with just seconds to spare.

They received a number *3* for their efforts, which meant as little to Elias as the last number, and somehow even less than the word puzzle from CYPHR's social media post. Deciding not to waste time pondering, Elias and Dakarai agreed to move on and go over the post and all their gathered clues after earning a few more.

Elias read the next one quietly to himself.

> ✉
> ### Random Act of Joy
> *Take a picture of something beautiful.*

Dakarai's head tilted upward toward the maze again, but his long lashes brushed against his cheeks as his eyes remained closed. This touched Elias. It wasn't often that others tried to see the world from his point of view.

In a maze more to his liking, Elias's eyes trailed down the slope of Dakarai's nose, resting on his lips for a moment before continuing down his neck, across his shoulders, and finally to the hand that hung freely at his side. Elias clenched his own fist, remembering just how surprisingly strong Dakarai's hand felt. Elias shut his mouth, catching himself gawking.

Without disturbing him, Elias discreetly captured a candid photo of Dakarai framed against the backdrop of the fire escape mural.

Dakarai turned around slowly, his eyes narrowed in suspicion. "Did you just take a picture of me?"

Without hesitation, Elias said, "You drew a picture of me. Why can't I take one of you?"

"Was it for a task?" Dakarai asked, craning his neck to peek at Elias's phone, which Elias held against his chest. Dakarai's smile broadened. "It was, wasn't it? Let me see."

Not wanting to repeat the struggle they'd had earlier over the drawing, he took a deep breath and handed over his phone.

"Take a picture of something beau—" Dakarai began but stopped short. He shifted and wrung his fingers together. "You don't mean that. People don't look at me the way they look at you."

"I don't even want to hear it." Elias folded his arms. "You don't remember the girl from work who wanted a comic recommendation? She took one look at you and left me with my book in my hand. You really don't think you're good-looking? If you don't say yes then you're a liar, and my mom warned me about boys like you."

"Fine, I do!" Dakarai said with a laugh. He took note of the new number, 5, then opened the next task.

> ✉
>
> **Random Act of Love**
>
> *Find a heart and take a picture of it.*

This one would probably be easy. The city felt like walking through the comic books that Dakarai loved so much. The buildings were low and made of brick, with mazes of telephone wires above them. The area was commercial, but there was artwork everywhere—everything from colorful murals and paintings to art installations to graffiti tags—gracing the sides of shops, schools, and even the sidewalks.

They kept walking, settling into a comfortable silence. Dakarai studied every piece of art, down to the sticker slaps on the backs of stop signs. Elias, however, kept his attention upward, thinking about what Dakarai had said earlier about the stars—how birth charts were a snapshot of the moment they were born and how the cosmos would never align that way again. With Elias's photographic memory, snapshots were something he knew well. Yet, he'd never considered them with such poetry before. Images from his entire life, starting with his earliest memories, were burned into his mind. The bad ones resurfaced when he least wanted them to, usually as he tried to sleep. But sometimes so did the good.

"It's a shame it's so late, isn't it?" Dakarai asked, pulling Elias out of his thoughts. Dakarai was several steps ahead, his eyes still scanning for a heart. "There are some really nice parks here and a rose garden. We should come back during the day and walk around them."

The corners of Elias's mouth lifted. "You're making future plans with me. We're real friends now, aren't we?" He quickened his pace to close the distance between them. "Admit it."

"We probably could be if you didn't talk so much," Dakarai said, rolling his eyes. A reluctant smile played on his lips.

Elias's smile widened. Dakarai truly seemed incapable of seeing anything but beauty in everyone and everything.

As they continued searching the street art for any signs of a heart, they passed by portraits of influential figures who seemed to be watching over them. Elias's favorite was a striking black-and-white mural of four legendary rappers painted on the side of a brick building next to a parking lot.

With his back to Kendrick Lamar, feeling the gritty coolness of the brick against his skin, Elias held up his phone and prepared to take a selfie. "Get in this with me."

Dakarai slid between Elias and the phone so they were face-to-face, nearly chest-to-chest. Elias recoiled slightly, surprised Dakarai was willing to get this close to him. Though the sudden proximity created an almost magnetic pull, and Elias felt himself drawn in by Dakarai's gentle-yet-commanding presence. The air grew thick, every breath and every heartbeat permeating the silence between them.

Lowering his phone, Elias mused, "Why aren't you afraid of me like everyone else is?"

Dakarai gave a noncommittal shrug. "You're not scary."

"Do I need to remind you why I'm even in North Carolina in the first place?"

"I can't see you getting into a fight, much less getting sent to a whole other state because of it. I know I don't know you well, but it doesn't feel like that's your character." Dakarai leaned in farther, and, for a moment, Elias thought Dakarai might kiss him. Elias inhaled sharply. Instead, however, Dakarai leaned against the painted brick next to him, adding, "It seems I haven't scared you off yet, either, by the way. That usually happens quickly."

Elias met Dakarai's eyes. "I'm afraid of the dark and you can't tie your shoes. We're not exactly two fish going in opposite directions, are we?"

They caught each other's gaze and held it for a while before they both looked away at the same time.

"I can't find a heart for this task, can you?" Elias asked.

A self-assured smirk flickered across Dakarai's face. He rested his palm on the left side of Elias's chest, giving it a few light pats, leaving Elias desperate to hold on to the moment. He closed the short distance between them, forming half a heart with his fingers, then beckoned Dakarai to complete the other side. But instead, Dakarai slid his hand up Elias's palm, opening it before intertwining their fingers. Elias's chest tightened, and he blinked hard trying to make sense of the gesture.

While Elias appreciated this particular piece of art, standing next to someone's Buick Enclave was throwing him off his game. It made no sense for him to be so flustered by such a small thing.

"I meant like this," Elias said, folding Dakarai's hand into shape, delicately, like origami.

Dakarai scratched the back of his neck and smiled shyly. "I knew that."

Elias snapped the picture of their heart quickly, giving Dakarai's hand a reassuring squeeze before reluctantly letting go.

He made a mental note of the new number, *8*—the reward for finding the heart—then tapped the new task.

> ✉
>
> **Random Act of Love**
>
> *Tell someone you love that you love them.*

Dakarai's expression was soft and discerning.

"It's too soon, don't you think?" Elias joked.

Narrowing his eyes at Elias, Dakarai replied, "I've got this one," as he pulled out his flip phone. His fingers moved swiftly over the keypad, pressing the "4" key three times with a soft *clack, clack, clack.* Then "5." *Clack, clack.* Then "6." *Clack, clack, clack.* Then "8." *Clack.* Then his finger jabbed on the "3" key. *Clack, clack.* And finally, "8" again. *Clack, clack.* He turned the phone around to show Elias, displaying I LOVE U in a text meant for Bobby.

With all the effort it took just to send one text, they must be *really* close.

Elias took Dakarai's flip phone to snap a picture as proof. Inadvertently, his eyes skimmed the previous few texts on the screen. He squinted, trying to stop himself from reading them, but they'd already imprinted in his mind.

KAI

FJSUWIZNPOKEGDPDDECCTW

BOBBY BAE

maybe a numeric anagram or cryptarithm?

KAI

my baby's so smart. Counting the days till we meet again

BOBBY BAE

you must go on without me

KAI

I LOVE U

Baby? Elias drew back in surprise. A feeling of betrayal stung his chest for a moment. The scavenger hunt was *their* thing. Why would he ask Bobby Bae? *He even has a cool name. Who the hell is this kid?* Elias thought. He'd never heard the terms *numeric anagram* or *cryptarithm* in his life.

Guiltily, he handed the phone back with a quick blurted confession. "I didn't mean to read your conversation," he said, "but, damn, if that's how you and your best friend talk, can I be your best friend too?"

Dakarai laughed it off, but Elias couldn't shake the text exchange from his mind. Elias had been so sure that Dakarai was warming to him and receptive of his advances, even reciprocating them at times. But if that's how Dakarai acted with Bobby, who's to say he wasn't just being friendly?

Dakarai wrote the number they received, *13*, on the back of his concert ticket along with the others they'd gotten so far. Elias then opened the next envelope.

> **Random Act of Kindness**
> *Write a poem for someone and record yourself reciting it.*

If there ever was a moment to make things right with Dakarai, it was this.

"I think there's an alternate universe version of me that's a SoundCloud rapper," Elias said, squaring his shoulders and rolling his neck in preparation. "Let me do this one."

Jogging a short distance to hop on top of the smooth surface of a tree stump with gnarled roots, he took a deep breath and tapped the record button. He held the phone steady as he aimed the front-facing camera at himself. Yet, his gaze remained fixed on Dakarai.

"You ready?" Elias asked, his voice lacking the usual self-assuredness everyone always accused him of having. He hesitated for another moment, running over the words in his mind before he began.

"I'll never be like Bobby Bae,

But I'm better in so many ways.

I can't define *cryptarithm*,

So maybe I can never be him.

But just . . . give me a chance, okay?"

Elias's jaw tensed slightly as he hit the stop button, his eyes immediately searching Dakarai's face for any hint of what he might be thinking. Elias leapt down from his makeshift soapbox. Flattery was a good start, but it wasn't enough for someone as kind and genuine as Dakarai.

"I'm sorry about earlier," Elias said resolutely.

"That could cover a whole bunch of things," Dakarai said. "Sorry about what specifically?"

Elias's phone chimed with a notification, but he toggled off the sound so it only vibrated. He took a steadying breath. "We never did talk about what happened at the bookstore," Elias said, prodding further. "You know, before Moodie the Mood Killer walked in."

"Nothing happened," Dakarai responded almost instantly.

"But if Moodie had walked in a minute later, would something have happened?" Elias watched Dakarai with anticipation.

"It doesn't matter," Dakarai responded. "You were just trying to piss off Moodie."

A sinking feeling struck Elias in the chest again. He wasn't saying things right. This had nothing to do with Moodie. He wanted to tell him that, but it was like his mouth was gummed shut. "I'm sorry" was all he could manage to say.

"I'm not," Dakarai replied, folding his arms over his chest. "It freed me. The old me would have named our grandkids already."

The two shared a brief chuckle that gradually faded into a tense silence.

"If I ever had a chance with you, did I ruin it?" Elias asked after a few moments. He shook his head slowly as he watched Dakarai hesitate to answer. "I ruined my chance with someone who is literally in love with the idea of being in love. This has got to be one of my greatest achievements."

It would have been easier if Dakarai were angry—anger he could understand. But the sheer disappointment on Dakarai's face somehow hit harder.

Elias, unsure of what else to do in this moment, brought out his phone and impatiently tapped on the notification he'd ignored earlier, hoping for a distraction, while Dakarai jotted down the number *21*.

> ✉️
> ### Random Act of Kindness
> *Give someone a compliment and record it.*

"I'll do this one." Dakarai took the phone, turning the camera on himself without breaking eye contact with Elias. "You're cute when you're sincere," he said, a smile tugging at the corner of his mouth as he handed the phone back.

"Okay, okay," Elias said, bowing his head to hide a smile of his own. *Buzz, buzz.* His phone vibrated in his pocket again, but he ignored it, too caught up in the moment. "I see I have more work to do, but you have to agree that this city would be a nice place for a date."

Dakarai's eyes lit up with a sudden attentiveness. "You think so?"

"Definitely. Of the two of us, you're the romantic. You tell me."

"I think it matters less about what you do and more about the person you do it with."

"So, roses and a box of chocolates wouldn't work for you, huh?"

"When someone gives me roses and a box of chocolates, I'll let you know."

"Noted. And for the record, I would take my date to the top of The Dalton for the view," Elias said pointing to the hotel where they'd been earlier that night. "And then we would take a walk through the Art District."

The neon light from a passing bus cast a soft pink hue onto Dakarai's face. His eyes shimmered as he asked, "Then what?"

"Maybe rent one of those scooters and see where else the night takes us," Elias said, gesturing to a few lime-green electric scooters parked at the corner. His smirk turned to a full smile when Dakarai laughed.

Buzz, buzz.

Another vibration in his pocket.

"You going to get that?" Dakarai asked.

"No."

Buzz, buzz.

"It's nothing important."

Music drifted in from the concert a few blocks away, reverberating off the nearby buildings to create a rhythmic backdrop. Swaying to the music, he playfully bumped into Dakarai with each motion.

Buzz, buzz.

"You sure you're not going to even check what it is?" Dakarai asked.

"It's probably the app yelling at me because I haven't opened the next envelope," he replied. "We don't have to open it just yet, do we?"

Dakarai raised an eyebrow. "I guess not," he replied. "But I will remind you that we're only doing this for you. I got to see CYPHR already."

Elias looked at him, daring Dakarai to slip into old habits and fall for him.

Buzz, buzz.

"You're doing all this to spend time with me," Elias said.

Dakarai's mouth dropped open in mock offense. "We have a whole summer of seven-hour shifts ahead of us. Why would I need to go through all this to spend time with you?"

"Because you know it's not enough."

Buzz, buzz.

"Just answer your phone already or turn it off!"

Elias sighed deeply. "Fine." He pulled out his phone, finally checking the most recent in a string of notifications:

10:45 PM

> Head to Second Chance Records for the biggest clue yet and a chance to access an exclusive unreleased track before the store closes at 11 p.m.!

10:50 PM

> Time is almost up! Can you make it to Second Chance before 11 p.m.?

10:55 PM

> Last call! Second Chance Records closes in 5 minutes.

10:58 PM

> Only a few minutes left to reach Second Chance Records. Don't let this clue slip away!

Elias blinked hard, only a single word tumbling from his lips. "Shit."

KAI

10:59 p.m.

Kai and Elias ran the block it took to get to Second Chance Records, glancing around nervously, hoping no one was watching them.

Throat raw and chest burning, Kai beat Elias to the door of the unassuming little shop, which was sandwiched between a corporate building and a hotel, with no differentiating features other than a small sign that'd be easy to miss if he didn't already know it was there.

At the exact moment Kai's fingers curled around the handle, relieved they'd made it on time, the familiar background sounds of the outdoor concert that had followed them all night abruptly went silent. "Good night, Ral—" was all the performing artist managed to say before her microphone was cut sharply, and the latch bolt clanged loudly within the doorframe—the disappointment of its rattle traveling through his body.

"Locked," Kai said, his chest heaving. "The eleven o'clock noise ordinance. We're too late."

"Shit," Elias said through heavy gasps of air as he crouched down, trying to catch his breath. "This is all my fault. I shouldn't have ignored my phone."

Kai scanned the store desperately, taking in the rows of records in raw plywood cases plastered with skateboard stickers and wheat-pasted posters, the reality of their failure not quite setting in yet.

"Elias!" Kai called when someone appeared from the back room, a middle-aged man with a full white beard, wearing a band tee.

With a semblance of hope restored, Kai stood optimistic. Elias, who had emerged beside him, did as well. The man came to the door and opened it only wide enough to stick his head out and say, "If you're here for the scavenger hunt, I'm 'fraid you're a little late."

Elias swallowed a gulp of the humid air and steadied his voice. "We won't tell anyone if you let us in," he said, twisting an imaginary key in front of his mouth and throwing it over his shoulder.

"I'm sorry, it wouldn't be fair to the other group I just turned away," he replied. "You boys have a good night."

"Wait!" Kai said before the door shut all the way. "It might not be fair, but the whole point of this scavenger hunt is to spread kindness and love, right? Maybe you could consider giving us a little break and showing my New Yorker friend here some of the Southern hospitality he keeps hearing about?"

The man was thoughtful for a moment before wordlessly relocking the door and disappearing behind a few shelves of records. Kai and Elias exchanged a glance, wondering if they'd been had. But a few moments later, the man returned, holding something in his hands—a metal device of some sort. "I can't let you in, but I don't see why I can't give you this," he said, handing Elias the object. "Maybe you can figure out how to open it without the clues inside the store. Not many people figured it out even with the hints, so good luck." With that, he shut the door, purposefully turning the lock with a loud *thunk*, the finality of which rang in Kai's ears.

"Thank you!" Kai yelled through the door, making a megaphone with his hands.

"For nothing . . ." Elias muttered under his breath as they examined the device. It was brass, shaped like a cylinder with a series of dials. "What the hell is this?"

A reverse image search told them it was called a cryptex.

"A cryptex is a kind of puzzle device made up of a series of rotating discs," Kai read aloud as Elias continued to fidget with it. *"Each disc features a letter of the alphabet. When aligned in the correct sequence, the puzzle device will open to reveal a hidden chamber inside, where a small item can be stored."*

"Did he give this to us as a joke?" Elias asked, trying to forcibly twist the discs. "I bet I can break it."

"Relax, it's not a pepper grinder," Kai said, "and it looks like it's already broken."

The discs were jammed and didn't turn smoothly. It seemed they had been overextended, and whatever internal components were inside were likely bent or broken.

"Great," Elias said, throwing his hands up in surrender. He sat down on the curb and folded his arms. "Not only do we not have the sequence to open the thing, but even if we did, it probably wouldn't work anyway."

"We still have some time left," Kai assured him. "CYPHR's post said we can figure out the location without this clue. Let's just keep doing the other tasks."

He sat beside Elias, and, together, they took inventory of all the numbers they'd earned so far: 0, 1, 1, 2, 3, 5, 8, 13, 21. Still, whatever message CYPHR was trying to get across wasn't obvious to Kai, and based on Elias's expression, it wasn't obvious to him either. Though he was still pouting, Elias did agree to continue on to the next task:

> ✉
>
> **Random Act of Mindfulness**
>
> *Your next location is one that isn't always there,*
> *But tonight, you're lucky to enjoy the open air.*
> *Head there before the sun makes it disappear,*
> *and absorb the history of Raleigh as you near.*

"We're still in the game," Kai said, nudging Elias lightly. "*Open air. Sun takes it away.* The answer is the Night Market. We have fifteen minutes to get there. Come on."

Elias kept his head hung low, not moving from where he sat on the curb.

Scanning the block until he spotted what he needed, Kai walked a short distance, lifted a scooter off its stand, and rolled it back to Elias.

"We can ride a scooter like you wanted," he said, trying to lift Elias's spirits. He placed Elias's phone in the handlebar holder for the GPS, then went over to Elias and gently tugged at his arm. "Come on. It'll be fun."

Elias reluctantly stood up, his arms remaining firmly folded. "How much time do we have?"

Kai smiled, glad to see Elias slowly warming. "Shall we?"

"Fine," Elias conceded. "But I want to be in front." He stepped onto the scooter, his back against the controls and elbows resting casually on the handlebars.

"Shouldn't you face forward?" Kai asked, stepping onto the back of the scooter.

Elias looked up at Kai with a playful smile. "I can't see you if I face forward," he said, motioning him closer. "And we'll be more aerodynamic if you come down here with me."

With a laugh, Kai put his arms on either side of Elias and positioned his head so his mouth was against Elias's ear. "This isn't part of the agreement."

"The agreement was that you get to know me," Elias said, the proximity of his voice making goose bumps erupt all over the back of Kai's neck. "This is me."

Elias's phone buzzed suddenly against his back, making him flinch violently like he'd had a bucket of cold water dumped down his shirt. He hid his apparent embarrassment at having been so easily startled in the curve of Kai's neck.

Trying to comfort him, Kai wrapped an arm around Elias. "Don't worry about the show, by the way," he cooed. "I'll ask Bobby. He knows everything."

"No," Elias said, raising his head suddenly. "Don't ask Bobby. I want *us* to figure it out."

It was clear Elias felt threatened by Bobby in some way, but Kai suspected it had less to do with Bobby and more to do with Elias's own pride. He'd seen the same reaction when the customer at the store had chosen Kai over Elias. Still, the jealousy intrigued Kai. No one had ever been jealous over him before. Though misguided, it was oddly flattering.

He only wanted Bobby's help so Elias could see CYPHR anyway, so with a nod, he agreed to keep the scavenger hunt between just the two of them.

They took off down the street together on the scooter, wobbling like a baby deer, and every time they hit even the slightest pebble or dip, it felt like they were about to flip over. Elias proposed that they each get their own wheels, keeping the scooter and leaving Kai with a bikeshare instead. Kai preferred the bike to the scooter but couldn't shake the feeling that he'd somehow offended Elias. Surely, Elias wasn't upset just because he'd suggested asking Bobby for help.

"Are you okay?" Kai asked Elias as they came to a traffic light. A car idled alongside, leaving him in a veil of exhaust when the light turned green.

"I'm good," Elias replied. He was back to reading off his usual script. *I'm fine. I'm good. I'll manage.* Though it was obvious he wasn't being entirely truthful, Kai didn't press. The thought of confronting Elias about being jealous, only to be wrong, would be an embarrassment he'd likely never recover from.

Downtown, the bars and restaurants were filling up with people who were eager to kick off the weekend with a few drinks and some good down-home cooking from one of the local late-night mom-and-pop spots. The air was thick with the saccharine aroma of maraschino cherries, the kind that lingered at the bottom of drained bourbon glasses. Kai pointed out the Raleigh Memorial Auditorium, the large state capitol building surrounded by statues of presidents, and the City of Raleigh Museum with its large metal globe at the entrance. Elias remained quiet, however.

They rode the rest of the way in silence until finally they came to the Night Market.

It was on a modest street, enclosed by zigzagging string lights suspended between two buildings. Canopy tents and tables adorned with various handmade crafts and goods lined the cobblestone street. Live music and the tempting smell of sweet treats coming from the food trucks mixed with the conversations and laughter of people shopping at vendor stalls or sitting on blankets in the grass.

Kai was drawn into the market like a cartoon character floating toward a pie on a windowsill. Though time was limited, he couldn't resist pausing at a few booths to compliment the vendors. As an artist himself, he understood how undervalued their work could be. Elias, however, seemed distracted, continuing to twist the cryptex and quickly showing Kai the number *34* and the newest quest the moment it appeared:

> ✉
> **Random Act of Honesty**
> *Make a confession.*

Kai glanced at Elias, hoping he had something to get off his chest—why he'd been so quiet, why he seemed to hate Bobby so much, if he really was serious about being sorry for earlier. But instead, Elias simply raised his phone, deadpan, and asked, "Do you have something?"

"Is it Sunday already?" Kai joked, though Elias only let out a short breath of laughter. Kai peered around at the others in the market, checking if anyone was paying attention. He swallowed, though his mouth was dry. "I guess I could make a confession," he said, his tone lower now. Waiting for Elias to start recording, he cleared his throat. "I confess . . . that I was warming up to you. More than I thought I would."

Elias immediately stopped recording and lowered his phone. He observed Kai through the corners of his eyes. *"Was?"*

Kai's hand went to the back of his neck. "You say you want to be friends, but I'm a little confused," he said. "For starters, you've been calling me Dakarai. You could try calling me Kai like everyone else does?"

135

A contemplative look settled on Elias's face. "You don't like your name?"

"Does everyone call *you* Elias, or do I have to complete some trials before you let me call you Eli like Moodie does?" Kai asked.

"You don't know how many times I've asked my family to stop calling me Eli," Elias replied. Spotting the confusion on Kai's face, he continued, "On my first day of kindergarten, my teacher, Ms. Townsend, kept calling me Eli, and I kept telling her that my name was Elias. You know what she said? She said that Elias was *too grandiose* of a name for a small boy. I didn't know what *grandiose* meant, but I knew I didn't like her tone, so since then, nobody calls me outside my name, and they can thank Ms. Townsend."

Kai bit his lip. He was starting to think that maybe, instead of hosing down the candle, he should have given Elias a good dousing, since he was clearly too hot-blooded for his own good.

"I just like your name," Elias continued, "and maybe I want to be the only one who says it."

A subtle blush crept across Kai's cheeks. Elias submitted the video, then recorded the number *55* before checking the next item:

Random Act of Kindness
Give a thoughtful gift.

"All this sentiment is making my head hurt," Elias groaned. His body shook with a sneeze, and his face contorted in pain. He lightly pinched the bridge of his nose and tilted back his head, closing his eyes as he sought relief.

"You're still hurt from the fight?" Kai said, as more of a statement than a question. He internally smacked himself for being so insecure. Elias wasn't upset with him. He was just in pain.

"No, I'm fine. I'll manage," Elias said, pulling down his hat farther, his eyes fixating on their shadows overlapping on the ground. "It's just allergies or a migraine or something. It looks like it's going to rain."

Stepping in front of Elias, Kai raised his hands and gestured to his face. He asked, "May I?" and added, "Don't worry. I won't hurt you," when he sensed Elias's apprehension.

Kai was sure Elias didn't fully understand what he was asking, but he nodded anyway, albeit hesitantly. Kai moved closer and placed his hands to the sides of Elias's face, pressing his thumbs gently to the pressure points beside his nose. He made sure not to touch the faint shadow of a bruise underneath Elias's eye that had begun to yellow and fade. As Kai massaged in a circular motion, Elias's face gradually relaxed. Kai felt a quiet sense of satisfaction.

"If I hadn't ignored those notifications, we'd probably be at the show by now," Elias said, his hand still firmly grasped around the still-jammed cryptex. "Do you think we'll ever figure out CYPHR's post?"

"We still have more clues to get through, so we can certainly try," Kai replied.

"You think there are one hundred people who are smarter than we are?"

"I think there are way more than one hundred people who are infinitely smarter than we are."

"You're probably right," Elias said as he stuffed the cryptex into his pocket and leaned closer into Kai's touch. "I just wanted to do something fun. I missed being in a city. Everything around your way is so quiet. How do you stand it?"

Elias joked a lot, but his honesty came in equal measure. He didn't show a ton of emotion, but he had a knack for dropping in little blink-or-you'll-miss-it truths like this. Elias didn't come off as the sentimental type, but he supposed anyone could get homesick. Kai had gotten homesick before he'd even gotten a chance to leave, so much so that he turned down his acceptance to Berkeley.

"How do *you* stand it? Big cities seem so chaotic and violent and impersonal."

"Maybe they are, but is it bad that I miss that?"

Kai gave a sly grin. "You think New York invented violence?"

"I mean, I guess not. I've seen your little Waffle House brawls," Elias teased.

"I know we're different. I grew up fishing and boating, jumping into rivers. I even went hunting a few times before I realized it wasn't for me."

"You? Hunting?" Elias asked incredulously.

"You think I came out the womb drinking oat milk?" Kai said dryly. "All I'm saying is that there's chaos in what you consider quiet," he continued. "For things to grow, something else has to die. But the violence and chaos you're talking about, the violence that bruised that pretty little face of yours—what grows from that?"

Elias held the tip of his thumb between his teeth, but he was unable to hide his amusement. "So you think I have a pretty face."

Kai released a slow exhale. "Don't let that be the only thing you take away from what I just said."

Elias gently placed his hands over Kai's to lower them. "All I'm hearing is that I still have a chance." Smiling warmly, he added, "I saw something at one of these tables you might like." He closed his eyes and tilted his head slightly, as if searching through memories. When his eyes snapped open, it was clear he'd found whatever he was looking for in his mind's eye. With a confident smile, he said, "Don't move. I'll be right back," before rushing off.

Kai watched as Elias slipped seamlessly into the crowd, weaving through the bustle. He stopped at a table they'd passed earlier, glancing back to meet Kai's gaze. With a quick, teasing wink, Elias sent a flush of heat rushing to Kai's cheeks. Kai looked down at his sneakers, trying to get himself together as Elias made his way back, a plastic bag held securely against his chest.

"Close your eyes and put out your hands," Elias urged.

Following Elias's instruction, Kai listened to the soft rustling of the bag, followed by the feeling of something rectangular being placed in his palm. The object was smooth to the touch, wrapped in a thin layer of plastic. When Kai opened his eyes and saw what it was, a genuine smile spread across his face.

"You got me tarot cards," Kai said in disbelief.

"The lady I bought them from said that she did the artwork herself," Elias said, his tone carrying a hint of embarrassment. "So if I see this shit on Canva, I'm coming back here." The way he spoke made it clear that he knew he'd done something thoughtful, even if the recognition for it was a little too much for him to bear.

Kai turned the deck over in his hands, his fingers tracing the box.

"I just don't think you should give up on your stars and tarot cards and stuff. I think it's cool," Elias said.

"You liked the palm reading, didn't you?" Kai asked.

"I like anything that leads you to me," Elias replied, his voice tender but sure. Kai swallowed hard. "Go on, then. Open it."

Elias took a picture of Kai as he ripped open the package and shuffled the deck. He did so, hand over hand, making sure to touch each card. Then he held the deck close to his chest and imbued it with his energy and intention. Once satisfied, he fanned out the cards, catching a swath of moonlight.

"Pick a card," Kai said, as more of a demand than a request.

Elias hesitated but obliged and said, "Don't tell me what it means right now. Tell me if it's true later."

Kai reflected on the card. Four of Wands. Elias's palm reading revealed that he deeply wanted something but didn't know what it was, but looking at this card, maybe what he wanted was stability. This card was more than that. It symbolized weddings, community, reunions, celebrations. Four of Wands symbolized solid foundations, coming home, and laying down roots.

I knew it, Kai thought, biting his lip to suppress a wide smile. For all of Elias's complaining about North Carolina, it was possible he was exactly where he needed to be. And maybe, just maybe, he was also put into Kai's life for a reason too.

Kai slipped the card back into the deck and pocketed it.

Elias raised an inquisitive eyebrow. "Is it a good one?"

Kai shrugged, a glint in his eye. "I guess you'll find out later."

"That's fine," Elias replied. "All I need right now is for you to do that pressure point thing again. Please?"

Elias stepped closer, guiding Kai's hands to his face. He shut his eyes softly.

Standing so near, their energies seemed to strike the same frequency. Everything around them dimmed and quieted, fading away until everyone else may as well have not even existed at all.

ELIAS

11:47 p.m.

Elias was completely lost in the moment. He nearly forgot where he was and what he was doing until Dakarai suddenly flinched. Concerned, Elias opened his eyes.

"Bathroom," Dakarai mouthed, attempting to excuse himself.

"Hurry back," Elias whined. Feeling much better thanks to Dakarai, he dreamily floated over to a nearby wall and leaned against it to wait.

Nia had always told him to open up more and be honest about his feelings. He'd never admit it to her face, but she was right.

He watched as Dakarai walked down a passage that led to the bathrooms. It was dark, which made it easy to notice when Dakarai pulled out his phone and held it to his ear, the glow of his screen illuminating his face.

Then it clicked—the thing that prompted this abrupt bathroom break was the vibration of Dakarai's phone.

The best friend, Elias thought, his curiosity lingering. He folded his arms, looking out over the thinning crowd. Even though he had initially wanted to spend the evening alone, now, with the absence of Dakarai's touch, isolation set in and he began to feel self-conscious.

"But I did everything right," he mumbled to himself. He'd listened to Nia and gone against every instinct to let his feelings about Dakarai be known—something he'd never done before. He'd been honest and vulnerable, given a thoughtful gift, and kept an open mind about all of Dakarai's interests that he normally would have belittled. And still, it wasn't enough.

Elias pressed his index fingers to the same spots Dakarai had, and the sinus pressure let up slightly so he could get one full breath of air. "Who takes care of me anyway?" he muttered.

Restless, he decided to text his little sister instead:

ELIAS
wake your ass up

He picked the skin around his nails, waiting for her to answer. Even though it was almost midnight, insomnia ran in the family, and she had a habit of pulling all-nighters to play computer games.

NIA
What do you want? 😒

He smiled inwardly. His relationship with Nia was the thing he was proud of most.

ELIAS
Nothing. I just wanted to see what you were doing.

NIA

I'm minding my own business.
What are you doing?

ELIAS

I'm talking to you. Don't you have
school tomorrow? Go to bed.

NIA

It's Friday. And it's summer.

ELIAS

Maybe you should go anyway. I saw
your last report card.

Before Nia could hurl another insult at him, he quickly typed out another text.

ELIAS

While we're talking, if you were on a date,
would you answer if someone called?

NIA

Only if it was an emergency. Why?
Are you striking out right now?

He cringed at the fact that he was asking his thirteen-year-old sister for dating advice—not that this was a date—but this was something he had never been good at. He'd had his first girlfriend in fifth grade, Xiomara Ruiz, and she had always accused him of yelling at her, despite him speaking in what he thought was his respectable inside voice. Now that he thought about it, the issue was probably him not using his respectable inside words.

ELIAS

You gonna give me any advice?
And don't tell me to be myself.

NIA

Be someone else, then. What did they
do to have you so pressed?

Elias thought a moment.

ELIAS

Do you remember that picture someone
drew of me that we found at the park
that one time? He's the one who drew it.

NIA

You're kidding. You stared at that
thing for weeks.

ELIAS

I know. Even though he left out my
most charming feature.

NIA

Your dimples? They're not that charming.

144

NIA

> And you probably weren't smiling, dummy.

A drop of water suddenly hit Elias's cheek. He wiped his mouth to make sure he hadn't spit, but then another drop fell, and then another. Looking up, he realized the drops had come from the sky and were quickly turning into a drizzle. It didn't take long for the situation to devolve into a downpour, drenching him.

He took cover at a table nearby, hopping on top of it to get as much protection under its umbrella as possible. The diamond pattern dug into his knee as he propped himself up to scan for Dakarai.

He tried calling Dakarai but got a busy signal. He tried again, and the call immediately dropped.

Elias grew anxious, afraid he wouldn't be able to find Dakarai when he came out of the bathroom. The umbrella, designed for shade and not rain, bowed and buckled under the weight, spilling curtains of water all around him, further obscuring his view. The people rushing for cover were indistinct dark shapes moving through the thick gray mist, as the café lights offered only a blurred glow.

He strained to keep an eye out for Dakarai, but it was getting even more difficult.

KAI

11:48 p.m.

Kai bit his lip and stared at his black phone screen for a moment. He awakened it, and his finger hovered over the green call icon.

"Why'd you answer? Aren't you still on your date?" Bobby asked as soon as Kai connected.

"Why'd I answer?" Kai echoed. "Why'd you *call*? And it's not a date . . . I don't think."

"I called to see if you were still out," Bobby replied. The excitement in his voice was evident.

Kai looked around to make sure no one was listening, as if he wasn't the only one in the bathroom stall. "I'm in crisis mode. It's going way too well."

"How can a date go *too well*?"

"I feel like I'm losing my mind," Kai explained in a rushed whisper. "I've been trying to play it cool, but you know me; I am *not* cool. I'm going to break any second, and he's going to realize how uncool I am."

"First of all, no one talks about my friend like that, even you. Second, I'm sure that's what he likes about you. Where is all this coming from? This morning, he was your twin flame. This evening, he wasn't. What is he now? You're giving me whiplash."

Kai left the stall. He leaned on the aluminum sink and hung his head. "If I'm being perfectly honest, I don't even think I care. I just like what we're doing."

From the constant joking and acting out, it was now clear to Kai that Elias was genuinely a happy person who just didn't get a lot of chances to be happy. They were both still kids, but it was evident that Elias didn't get many opportunities to act like one. All Kai had wanted for years was to be noticed first, to be liked first, for someone to chase him for once—and there Elias was.

"I like you like this," Bobby said. "Now get off the phone with me and go hang out with your new boyfriend."

"He's not— I'm too scared. How did you know that you liked Winter?"

"I'm still not sure I do," Bobby whispered.

"I can hear you!" Winter's voice sounded in the background.

"I guess it's back to the farmers market for you, bro," Kai said with a strained chuckle. "Why don't you make me a pie with all those apples?"

"Only my nice friends deserve pie," Bobby retorted.

"Yeah, whatever. Bye."

He closed his phone and put it in his pocket. Anxiously, he tugged at the braid hanging in front of his face. He couldn't help smiling to himself, but, because he was alone, he felt ridiculous, so he stopped.

"What am I doing hiding in here?" he asked himself. "Bobby's right."

When Kai stepped out of the bathroom, he was met with a light drizzle. He huddled beside a vending machine. Pulling a crumpled dollar bill from his pocket, he used the corner of the machine to carefully flatten it before feeding it into the slot.

Coke in hand, he looked out over the Night Market as the rain got progressively heavier. Elias wasn't where Kai had left him. He'd probably sought shelter like everyone else, ducking under awnings or into nearby shops, or making a run for the buses or their cars.

"Where are you?" Kai muttered as his eyes continued to comb the market, but it was hard to see almost anything.

He pressed his phone to his ear, but it went straight to voicemail.

"No signal," he muttered to himself.

Panic began to creep in. He took a few deep breaths, steeling himself, then charged out into the rain. His clothes were instantly saturated, water streaming down his back, seeping into his mouth and eyes. Cold water crept into his shoes as he pinballed around the market, desperately searching for Elias. But the downpour was too much for the makeshift visor he'd created with his hand, and the squish of his waterlogged tennis shoes slowed him down with each step.

Retreating beneath a metal canopy at the entrance of a closed restaurant, Kai began emptying his pockets to assess the rain's damage to his belongings. His phone, keys, wallet, and folded concert ticket were all soaked, but the deck of tarot cards remained safe, neatly wrapped in a plastic bag. He shook the water from his phone and tried to power it on, but it stayed dark.

He didn't know what to do. He couldn't call Elias. He couldn't go home. And he certainly couldn't stay here.

A clock overlooking the market square struck midnight as Kai watched. The secret CYPHR show had already started.

Gently peeling apart his wet concert ticket, he revealed the numbers he and Elias had scribbled down during the scavenger hunt. He paused, thinking. Maybe his best chance of reuniting with Elias was at the show. He hoped Elias had the same thought.

ELIAS

11:56 p.m.

With his nail polish scratched nearly all the way off, Elias finally decided Dakarai was taking too long. He inhaled the thick, humid air, then ran out into the deluge. With determination, he knocked on the bathroom door and pulled it open when no one answered. It was empty.

How did he pass by me without me noticing? Elias thought.

Elias went back to the center of the square and spun around. Dakarai was nowhere in sight.

Eventually, he became overwhelmed by the sheer force of the rain and darted into a bus shelter, sitting on the bench as he wrung out his shirt and emptied his shoes, joining a few others who were doing the same. He tried calling Dakarai again, but it went to voicemail. *Is he still talking to Bobby?* Unsure of what to do next, Elias waited. For what, he did not know.

A bus pulled up, and everyone except Elias boarded. The driver glanced at him in confusion, shrugging before driving off.

Even though he had initially wanted to spend the evening alone at the concert, now that he'd spent the day with Dakarai, all he wanted was to be in his company. In the span of about fourteen hours, they'd gone from almost-strangers to coworkers, to possibly friends, to whatever it was they were now. Elias couldn't help but wonder if they'd be strangers again tomorrow.

He watched the rain pelt the ground around him. This was not a quick shower, and it seemed unlikely to let up anytime soon.

He glanced at the time—12:01 a.m. The secret show had already started. If he had been trying to fix the cryptex instead of just fiddling with and complaining about it, they might be at the show by now, rather than separated in the rain.

He struggled to twist the cryptex, which still resisted with a slight scraping noise. Lifting it to his ear, he tried to locate the obstruction. Finally, he pulled out one of his earrings and inserted the post into the seam between two of the dials where he felt resistance. It dislodged something, and the dials turned smoothly this time. Carefully, he rotated the dials, feeling for any hesitation or change. Nearly completing the entire alphabet, he heard a soft click. He listened closely, rocking the cryptex back and forth as it clicked almost imperceptibly. He identified the first letter in the sequence as *C* and repeated the process with the other four dials, straining to hear the same subtle click amid the rain pounding overhead. After several minutes, the last dial clicked into place with a satisfying sound, and he smiled.

Holding the cryptex in front of him, he revealed the letters spelled out *CYPHR*.

"You've got to be kidding me," Elias muttered, placing his palm on his forehead.

Gingerly, he pulled one side of the cryptex, and it slipped open, revealing a small chamber inside. He tipped it into his hand and found a flash drive. It undoubtedly contained the file for the exclusive unreleased song.

Turning it over, he saw an engraving on the back: "FIBONACCI" WRITTEN AND PERFORMED BY CYPHR.

As he closed his eyes, he visualized the numbers he and Dakarai had collected throughout the night. Then he looked at the assortment of letters from CYPHR's original post. Realization set in as he reviewed them—it seemed he was going to that show after all. He just prayed Dakarai would be able to figure it out too.

KAI

12:11 a.m.

Kai glanced at the clock again: 12:11. He chuckled to himself. Those were his and Elias's seat numbers at the concert. It reminded him that he had seen the number eleven repeatedly that day and in the days leading up to meeting Elias—on clocks, street addresses, license plates, his damage score on *Guild Wars*, the bus to Raleigh, their concert seats. Suddenly, a light bulb went off in Kai's head. His mouth dropped open as he remembered that Elias had selected the Four of Wands from the tarot deck. The card reflected four wooden pillars, two on each side: *11:11*.

"Oh my God. The golden ratio," Kai said, slapping a palm against his forehead with a laugh. He was an artist. He should have thought of this sooner.

FJSUWIZNPOKEGDPDDECCTW

Kai studied the letters from the post again, trying his best to preserve the soggy piece of paper. He compared the letters against the series of numbers they'd collected by completing the tasks in the scavenger hunt.

0, 1, 1, 2, 3, 5, 8, 13, 21, 34

"It's the Fibonacci sequence," Kai murmured, his smile growing wider.

The Fibonacci sequence was everywhere—in nature, human anatomy, music. It started with zero—nothing—followed by a *1*, then another. Zero symbolized the soul, while the double ones represented the two parts that comprised a single soul. That's why the pillars were 11:11 and not 1:1. This was why 11 was the most important number in the world of twin flames, and Elias just so happened to pull it from the deck. Kai was hesitant to call this fate, but when things aligned so perfectly, what else could it be? Even Elias had told him not to give up on his stars and tarot. If Kai had, he would've missed this rare moment in which art, science, and the divine came together in harmony.

He considered the letters on the soggy paper for a moment: *FJSUWIZNPOKEGDPDDECCTW*. It was probably a simple shift cipher. All he had to do was take each letter and shift it by the numbers in the sequence. He began, scratching the decoded message onto his palm with his fingernail as though they were a pen and pad: *F* shifted by 0 stayed as *F*, *J* shifted by 1 became *K*, *S* shifted by 1 became *T*, *U* shifted by 2 became *W*, and *W* shifted by 3 became a *Z*.

Letting out a frustrated sigh, Kai wished his mind worked a little more like Elias's. Better yet, he wished Elias were there. Holding all the letters and numbers in his head without writing them down was tough. He paused to think over what he'd decrypted so far.

FKTWZ? he thought.

He ran every possible calculation that his left brain could manage, but even knowing the cipher was created using the Fibonacci sequence, the letters still weren't making sense.

"I was so sure of it," Kai said, pressing a knuckle into his right temple. He wanted to call Bobby, but his phone had broken in the rain. "I can figure this out without him," he said. That's what Elias had wanted.

And just like that, Kai's faith was restored. He had to shift the numbers backward, not forward.

FIRSTDRAUGHTSECRETSHOW

His eyes widened. First Draught was a venue only a few blocks away—a record store by day and a bar by night.

Kai sprinted out into the torrent.

ELIAS

12:13 a.m.

Elias's feet slapped against the wet sidewalk as he ran down the street. He squinted as water rushed into his eyes, making it difficult to read the store signs. They'd walked past First Draught earlier in the night. He just had to keep following the map in his mind.

Finally, he spotted it—a squat brick building painted black. Elias's heart pounded in his ears as he half expected to see Dakarai waiting there for him in the rain. All that greeted him when he got near were windows completely plastered with posters from old concerts, skateboard stickers, and vinyl record covers, and the growing roar of the storm. He knelt down to peer inside through a small, foggy gap.

"Where is he?" Elias muttered. He should have stayed put—if he had, they'd be inside right now—dry, warm, and, most importantly, together.

Elias felt a pang of regret that was instantly replaced by a chill down his spine when someone tapped on his shoulder. Elias spun around to find Dakarai standing there, drenched, his clothes clinging to his body. Rain droplets streamed down his face, tracing the curve of his jaw, down his throat, and along his collarbones. A sudden surge of excitement charged the air, and Elias instinctively reached for Dakarai, who reached for him back. For the briefest moment, quicker than a single heartbeat, it seemed that their lips might meet in a celebratory kiss. Instead, Elias cupped Dakarai's cheek, holding on to him like he'd been searching for him for the last five years, since finding that crumpled portrait in the park, and not just since the Night Market. Elias's soaked clothes made him hyperaware of every sensation, from the trickle he felt leaking down the back of his neck to the warmth he felt coming from Dakarai's hands on his waist.

Elias blew the rain from his mouth. "You figured it out on your own?"

"I did. Just like you asked me to," Dakarai said, almost in a whisper, as if he was running out of breath. "How did you do it?"

"I hacked the cryptex. But where did you go?"

"You got me a thoughtful gift, and I wanted to get you something too. It's stupid though," Dakarai said, holding up a can of soda.

Elias narrowed his eyes in confusion—he didn't recall telling Dakarai he was thirsty. Still, he reassured him, saying, "It's not stupid."

Gently, Dakarai pressed the can against the bridge of Elias's nose, with the heel of it resting neatly in the hollow of his eye. The chill provided a quick reprieve, making him realize just how much the headache had been bothering him. The gesture was so simple, so sweet, and so on-brand for Dakarai. It warmed Elias, and for a moment, he forgot just how cold he had been and how hopeless he'd felt only minutes before.

"You could have just kissed it better," Elias said with a forced laugh.

Without missing a beat, Dakarai lowered the can and leaned in closer. His ragged breath matched Elias's own. Instinctively, Elias shut his eyes, knees buckling as Dakarai's lips grazed the spot where he'd been struck just a week ago. Dakarai planted a soft kiss, then another, and another. "We've got the rest of the night," Dakarai rasped, leaving one final kiss lingering on the lid of Elias's eye. "Let's get out of this rain."

Elias nodded. It was all he could do.

KAI

12:29 a.m.

Kai watched as Elias wrenched open the door, inviting Kai to go inside first before following, using his hands like windshield wipers to brush water from his arms and legs. Elias wrung out his hat and then wiped his feet on the rug.

The small venue was only a solid black room with bright stage lights overhead. The stage was all the way in the back, with two bars on each side and walls covered completely by black curtains. The upstairs area was roped off, but a few shelving units containing vinyl records could be seen through the metal railings.

"Wait, come here," Kai said, pulling Elias back by the waist before he went to the ticket counter. He straightened out Elias's hat and smoothed down his shirt before wiping a trickle of water from his cheek with his thumb.

Elias looked up with lazy smile. "Did that feel real back there?" he asked.

"What?" Kai replied.

"Earlier, you said that what might have happened at Uncle Moodie's wouldn't have been real. Is it real now?"

Craning his neck, Kai leaned down until they were only a breath apart. Elias closed his eyes in anticipation. "Yes," Kai said as he playfully shook his head, spraying Elias as water flew from the ends of his hair.

"Tickets!" a woman seated at the desk shouted over the music, startling Elias.

Kai laughed as he urged Elias forward. He whined as he wiped his screen against his pants, then handed his phone over to the woman. "How many people have figured out the scavenger hunt?" he asked.

"You're number ninety-nine and one hundred," she said as she looked over his ticket. "Congratulations," she added dryly.

Pride flashed over Elias's face, and he turned back and winked at Kai.

He stood on his tiptoes as he waited for Kai, seemingly trying to catch a glimpse of CYPHR over everyone's heads. But from all the way back here, the entire stage was pretty much washed out by the stage lights, and there were a few support beams in the way. They could only hear CYPHR.

Kai reached into his pocket and pulled out the remains of his paper ticket. He tried to open it up, but it crumbled under the weight of its own sogginess and disintegrated in his hands.

"Do you have a digital ticket?" the woman asked, her expression flat as she eyed what was now a wad of pulp. "Proof of purchase for CYPHR's canceled show is required."

"If you give me a moment."

"Too late. Looks like you're numbers one hundred and one and one hundred and two," she said, waving in another soaking-wet duo who hurried in from the rain.

Elias slid in front of them and said, "He showed you his ticket."

"I have to be able to scan it. Those are the rules."

A young man wearing a security T-shirt approached. "We're at capacity. If you'd please step outside, unfortunately, once you're out, re-entry isn't possible, even with a ticket."

"Joshua?" Elias said, his eyes taking on a glimmer of hope.

"*Joshua?*" Kai puzzled aloud. "Wait, Joshua from the bus stop?"

Elias's fast friend from earlier that night, the gym rat. Kai supposed this is what he meant when he said he worked in security. He'd initially assumed Joshua had meant cybersecurity or law enforcement, but this certainly qualified as well.

"Sorry, Elias," Joshua said, his expression still blank. "I can't let you guys in."

"Come on, you know me, man. You can vouch for us."

Joshua appeared to have said all that he was going to say. He simply folded his arms and looked at the two of them with a menacing glare.

Of course, Kai thought with a mental facepalm. *Elias would make friends with a human biceps.*

"You can tell the lady to ask nicely, and we'll leave," Elias said, folding his arms over his chest to mirror Joshua.

He could hear the two whispering to each other for a moment before the woman said, "Would you be so kind as to step outside? *Please.*"

"No," Elias replied with a snicker.

She made a motion, and Joshua advanced.

Elias held up his hands defensively. "Fine. Relax. Just give us a minute." They appeared shocked that he'd relented so easily. "Expect a zero-star review, though. I thought we had something special, Joshua!" Elias shouted as he yanked his bucket hat over his eyes and opened the door. "Did you hear, everyone? This place is haunted and has rats!"

A few people standing at the back of the crowd looked in his direction but quickly dismissed him.

He proudly waved his middle fingers like flags as he and Kai exited the building with nowhere to go.

They paused in the doorway, trying to come up with a plan. Through the glass, Joshua and the ticketing woman had a united front, their body language screaming *You don't have to go home, but you have to get the hell up out of here.*

Elias raised a hand to Kai before he could say anything. "I realize I lost control of that situation."

"You did . . . but thanks."

A nervous laugh escaped Elias's lips.

As if he could read his mind, Elias counted to three, and they both sprinted around to the side of the building. Next to the entrance, there was a black awning over the door, and they ducked under it to escape the rain. The rain drummed against the vinyl awning and cascaded down its sides like a sheet, forcing them to huddle in about three square feet of dryness. They moved closer to avoid the rain splashing up from the ground that misted their ankles.

Kai wanted to write a thank-you letter to the rain to personally thank it for being the best wingman imaginable.

"I can hear him," Elias said, pressing his ear to the door. Kai also pressed his ear to the cold steel, and CYPHR's set was faint but certainly audible. He didn't lament not being inside, though; he liked his current view. He watched as Elias's pupils expanded and his face lit up every time CYPHR hit a guitar riff he liked or the crowd cheered. The only thing Kai wanted to cheer for was this moment.

ELIAS

12:48 a.m.

When their necks became sore from standing in awkward positions, the two took a seat beside each other on the stoop, leaning their heads back against the door and listening to the music.

"You have your ticket; you can probably still charm your way in," Dakarai urged. "I promise I don't mind."

"You didn't leave me at the bus station earlier; I'm not going to leave you now. This isn't exactly how I pictured us getting rewarded for cracking the code, but this is nice."

"It is," Dakarai agreed.

Their moment was interrupted by two squealing girls crossing the street, using their hands and purses to cover their hair as they ran toward Elias and Dakarai.

"I'm sorry, can we hide under here with you?" one of them asked.

The boys got to their feet and huddled together so the girls could join them under the awning.

"Oh my God, thank you so much. Where did this rain even come from? I'll be shocked if any of my makeup is still on my face," the other girl said. Her large deep-set eyes were the most striking feature of her face, and her lashes were so full and long that they nearly met her thick brows. "I'm Sarita and this is Imani." She pointed to Imani, who was trying to shield her natural hair from the mist of water that persisted under the covering.

"Here you go," Elias said, offering Imani his hat. Her dark eyes and dark skin glistened in the rain.

"Lifesaver," she said, immediately tucking her hair into the hat and yanking it down as low as she could. "Thank you."

"You both are here for the concert?" Sarita asked.

Elias let out a sigh. "We misplaced our tickets, so they wouldn't let us in. We're just trying to wait out the rain."

"Was the person at the front a woman with a really tight pony-tail and no laugh lines in sight?"

Elias and Dakarai gave each other a knowing look before Elias responded with "That's the one. You know her?"

Sarita nodded. "My girlfriend works here, and she complains about her all the time. Her name's Robin."

"*Robin*," the four of them repeated with disdain.

The door suddenly swung open, and the group was thrust back into the rain. They got completely soaked all over again by the wall of water, resulting in a collective groan.

"Oh my God, I'm so sorry. Get in here," the person who'd opened the door said, waving them in.

Imani handed Elias's hat back and said, "Thank you," before ducking inside.

"Thanks so much for sharing the covering with us," Sarita said as she was pulled inside by, presumably, her girlfriend.

Just before the door closed, Dakarai said, "Wait!" Sarita stuck her head back out. "Do you—this is going to sound kind of awkward, but do you guys want to be friends?" Dakarai shot an uncertain glance at Elias. "There's only, like, an hour left of the show. Any chance we can come in with you?"

He remembered the side quest, Elias thought with a proud grin planted firmly on his face.

"Hang on, I'll be right back," Sarita said. The door shut with a metal click. Elias and Dakarai shrugged at each other, but Elias couldn't hide how impressed he was with Dakarai's boldness.

The door swung open again, forcing them back out into the rain.

"Did I seriously do that again?" Sarita asked, horror washing over her face. She slid out, mindful of keeping a hand on the doorjamb so the door wouldn't shut. "So, the bad news is that my girlfriend said I can't let you in. But the good news is that this door closes really slow, and I can't be expected to watch it until it closes all the way, can I? I don't even work here, so that's above my pay grade. Sound good?"

"Yes, yes! A thousand times yes!" Elias said, clasping his hands together over his heart.

She laughed, and then, with a fervent push, the door flung wide open, releasing a rush of sound into the night. Elias grabbed the door and held it ajar but paused for a moment.

"What's wrong?" Dakarai asked.

"You completed the dare," he replied. "I said you could have anything you wanted." Elias ran his other hand over the top of his head and swallowed hard. "Well . . ."

Dakarai pulled Elias toward him by the waist. He blinked hard, completely at a loss for words as his lips parted in anticipation. Dakarai searched Elias's face for permission. Elias raised his head as far as he could without letting his heels leave the ground. Permission granted. Dakarai grasped the side of Elias's face and indulged his expectant mouth with a short but deliberate kiss.

Dakarai drew back and said, "I've already gotten what I've wanted all night."

Elias had been needed plenty, but *wanted*? This felt new. Internally, he was kicking his feet. *He wants me?* he thought, repeating it with more self-assurance. *He wants me.*

Dakarai maintained a hold on Elias's waist as they walked inside, maneuvering through the black, dimly lit corridor past people headed toward the bathrooms. The passageway muffled the sounds of the concert, choking it off at the entrance and offering some relief from the volume. Dakarai stopped Elias by the arm there, out of view of security, and leaned him up against the wall as people rushed by behind him, pressing them farther together.

Elias picked at what was left of his nail polish, betraying his nerves. Dakarai didn't seem nervous at all as he leaned over and took Elias's face in his hand, resting the heel of his palm against the hollow of his throat. Dakarai nudged his nose with his own to tilt Elias's head. Lingering there for a moment, Elias was expectant, though he was only indulged millimeters at a time. Then, without further warning, Dakarai leaned in all the way. As they kissed, Dakarai's hand slid up Elias's neck, and his thumb followed the line of Elias's jaw, his fingers making a circular motion on his earlobe the same way he did to himself when he was anxious.

Even though Elias wanted what was happening more than he'd ever wanted anything in a long time, he could hear a familiar voice creeping into his brain. He had always been a fighter, not a lover. What made him think he could be what Dakarai needed and wanted? Dakarai had been very clear that he was not one whose emotions should be toyed with. Was Elias doing something wrong? As he leaned farther into this kiss, Elias noticed that something was, in fact, different this time. He didn't have that pit in his stomach he got when he was talking back, or picking fights, or doing anything he knew he shouldn't be doing but just couldn't stop himself. He felt at ease, a sense of calm washing over him, like he had finally found his way home.

Dakarai finally pulled away, leaving Elias breathless and with stars in his eyes.

"Are you okay?" Dakarai asked, cradling him in his hands as though he might break—as if he could sense Elias retreating into his head.

Elias nodded.

He wished Dakarai had introduced himself all those years ago in the park, but at the same time, it wasn't likely he was ready to receive him then. Tonight could have only happened tonight.

His gaze wandered beyond Dakarai, and Elias suddenly became aware that they weren't the only two in the room. He made eye contact with someone who began making their way over to them.

Dakarai hid his face for a moment, seemingly to fix himself, before turning around to greet Sarita and Imani. They were heckling them for their cuteness, eliciting a nose scrunch from Elias and a broad, toothy smile from Dakarai.

"We saw you made it inside and thought we'd get our new friends some drinks to celebrate," Sarita said, extending two of their four shot glasses to Dakarai and Elias. The boys shared a smile before taking them. They were filled to the brim with a red liquid that looked like juice. Elias raised it to his nose and sniffed. It smelled like juice too.

Elias slurped the excess off the top of his so it didn't spill. "Mmm. What are they?" he asked, the glass hovering near his lips.

Imani leaned in to answer. "They're called Swedish Fish shots."

"*Swedish Fish?!*" Elias repeated, snatching the glass right out from under Dakarai's nose in one smooth motion. "We're good.

Underage, in fact. See? No hand stamp." Elias pointed to the back of his right hand.

Dakarai chewed on the inside of his mouth as he bit back a laugh.

"Suit yourself!" Sarita sang before she and Imani downed all four shots back-to-back, then headed to the dance floor.

CYPHR grasped at his mic with his eyes closed as he sang in falsetto, and his band accompanied him on an all-acoustic version of the first song of CYPHR's that Elias had ever heard. The crowd went alight, a hundred swaying cell phones popping up one by one to match the slower tempo and softer sounds. The only one who wasn't transfixed was Elias. He couldn't keep his eyes off Dakarai with his profile backlit by the red stage lights, which accentuated the contours of his face. Elias knew it wouldn't take long for Dakarai to feel his stare.

"What's on your mind?" Dakarai asked, finally turning to look at Elias.

"You never told me what my tarot card was earlier."

"The Four of Wands, which represents celebration, joy, and a sense of homecoming. Does any of that resonate with you?"

Elias bit the inside of his cheek. "I think it does."

He nestled his chin on Dakarai's shoulder, taking the fabric of Dakarai's shirt between his teeth and, with playful determination, attempted to draw him closer by the collar.

Dakarai tapped on his chest, signaling for Elias to rest his head against him. When he did, Dakarai draped his arm protectively across Elias's chest, and finally, they watched the show.

"I swear I'm not usually like this," Elias said, "but you bring it out in me."

"Same," Dakarai replied, his voice resonating against Elias's back.

A goonish smile settled on Elias's face, and he melted farther into Dakarai. Sinking into a relaxed stupor, Elias felt the tiredness from the day finally taking over as he watched CYPHR perform.

♪ If we kiss once, we can't take it back
But if we kiss this once, I can kiss you again ♪

"This song has been stuck in my head for weeks," Elias said.

"It's my favorite," Dakarai replied. "I'm glad I got to hear it live, finally."

CYPHR commanded the small stage. Bathed in the glow of stage lights, against the black muslin, he moved with a confidence that was apparent in every gesture. He handed off his guitar to a bandmate before settling in front of a keyboard to play a ballad version. The audience was captivated by CYPHR as he lost himself within his music.

Elias tapped the beat with his fingertips against Dakarai's arm. They were still soaking wet, and under any other circumstances, they would have been completely miserable. However, with the bass pounding in their chests, they didn't even notice that their clothes were sticking to them. They didn't care that they'd have to be at work in the morning. Elias hadn't felt this way in a long time—perhaps ever. The only thing that could make this moment even better was getting closer to CYPHR.

Elias gave Dakarai's leg a playful squeeze. Leaning close to Dakarai's ear, he said, "Let's go join everybody else."

"We'll get kicked out if your best friend Joshua sees us."

"It's, like, two in the morning. I want to get kicked out," Elias said, extending his arm to Dakarai.

Elias half expected that he'd need to convince Dakarai more, but he was surprised and delighted when Dakarai motioned for him to lead the way. Was it possible that Elias brought out Dakarai's boldness?

ELIAS

1:50 a.m.

As the two neared the stage, the venue started to look more like a private party than a club. The bass rising in Elias's chest was almost unbearable, as though it had replaced his own heartbeat. Rotating red lights cast long, sensual shadows that moved in rhythm to the music. Every inch of the room was bathed in red light, which clung to the veil of fog that fell from somewhere above. The sun could have been up and people could have been on their way to church for all he knew. Walking into that red den was like entering into a vacuum where time was only a suggestion.

Elias led Dakarai by the arm through the sultry red glow. As he stepped closer to the stage, it was like figures appeared in the mist, looking him up and down. Some of their eyes lingered on him, but most drifted behind him to Dakarai.

It was so much louder on the floor than it had been in their little tucked-away corner. The sheer volume felt confining, and Elias stopped—they'd gone far enough. He wrapped Dakarai's arms around his waist and leaned his head back onto Dakarai's shoulder. His body completely lost all strength the moment Dakarai held him, and he closed his eyes for a moment as they swayed together, watching the red-drenched CYPHR with the silhouettes of hundreds of hands against him, tendrils of fog shining through their fingers.

One hundred heads pointed their chins toward the ceiling at the sound of a loud pop. Confetti gushed from above. The band then launched into their next song, spraying bottles of water into the audience.

The cool droplets hit Elias's skin, awakening and exhilarating him. He turned to face Dakarai, who was shaking the confetti from his hair. With a touch as gentle as a whisper, Dakarai cradled Elias's face in his hands, his fingers delicately wiping away the liquid that threatened to fall into his eyes.

Then Dakarai's eyes suddenly grew wide, and Elias watched as he ducked down as if trying to shrink himself. Elias followed his gaze and was met with the familiar eyes of the security guard, his short-lived friend, Joshua. Stationed near the entrance, Joshua's stoic demeanor turned from confusion to rage in an instant. He knelt to talk to Robin. What they were saying was inaudible, but Joshua was pointing directly at Elias, punctuating every word with a deeper furrow of his brow.

Elias put his mouth to Dakarai's ear so he could hear him over the rattling bass and said, "Let's go."

As they scurried away, Dakarai accidentally bumped into a woman wearing a men's hoodie that went down to her knees. He quickly said sorry, but she shoved Dakarai back and clung on to the man next to her, who was presumably her boyfriend, with a fervent "Fuck you!"

"Stay away from my girl," the boyfriend said.

"Stay away from your girl?" Elias repeated incredulously, jumping in front of Dakarai. "You thought he was trying to be

your boyfriend-in-law? He was just trying to get past."

"Let's just calm down," Dakarai said, his eyes scanning the room nervously for Joshua.

"I'll calm down when he says sorry," the boyfriend said, pointing at Dakarai.

In a room too small for the sound being created inside of it, the boyfriend's voice was the thing causing Elias's temples to throb. He had chosen the hour just before sunrise, on a night when no one had had even a wink of sleep, and everyone was soaked with rain and confetti, to throw a tantrum.

Elias gave an apologetic look to Dakarai, who probably wasn't going to like what he was about to do.

"He already said sorry," Elias said. "And he wasn't hitting on her. We're together."

The boyfriend scratched his head. "What do you mean?"

"What do you mean *what do you mean*? The two of us are on a date, as in with each other, and no one's trying to talk to your girlfriend. Now turn your goofy ass around and leave us alone."

Elias, chest puffed and shoulders high, felt a strong sense of pride for not swinging at this guy. Perhaps the influence of Southern kindness was already starting to rub off on him. As he turned to Dakarai, seeking his well-deserved pat on the back, Elias found his attention usurped by something entering his periphery fast. Muscle memory alone propelled him backward in a clean dodge, only to discover that the boyfriend's attempt to throw his drink on Elias had backfired in spectacular fashion. The unintended consequence being that Dakarai, not Elias, was now the one wearing an assortment of melting ice cubes.

It was only a week ago that Elias took a hit to the face from a preteen, albeit one who looked like he was on a steady diet of red meat and other people's lunches. And while he usually prided himself on his facial symmetry, he really wasn't trying to get a knock to the other side. He wasn't that person. It's likely he never was. Or at least he didn't want to be anymore, especially here, with Dakarai.

Elias pinched the bridge of his nose and let out an exasperated sigh. "I did it again, didn't I?"

"No one got hurt," Dakarai said, brushing the ice off.

Wanting to prevent an impending altercation, Elias grabbed Dakarai's hand, and they broke away from the disgruntled couple, nearly taking a head dive into the black waters of the floor, which was slick with spilled drinks. They wove through the dancing bodies on the dance floor, shimmied between couples, ducked behind an empty DJ booth, and eventually made it to the back hallway that led to the bathrooms. Elias looked all around for Joshua, but he was no longer in sight. He yanked Dakarai by the arm, and they both got into a half squat.

"What are *you* squatting for?" Dakarai asked.

"Solidarity. Just stay down," Elias shouted over the music.

"Well, what's the plan? We can't duck them forever."

"Let's just go out the door we came in. It's probably time we got home anyway."

Elias and Dakarai exchanged a tacit pep talk in the form of firm nods. Elias then led the way into the dark passageway, only to reemerge about ten seconds later slung over the shoulder of his former friend Joshua, Dakarai in tow.

Elias observed CYPHR getting smaller and smaller past Dakarai's head as he was carried out. He felt like a popped parade balloon hanging limply over Joshua's shoulder. As such, he waved goodbye to Imani and Sarita, who were at the bar. Joshua escorted Elias and Dakarai all the way to the main doors, where they walked past Robin, who wasn't made any more pleasant by the last few hours that had passed.

"We could have been great friends, Joshua," Elias said as his feet met the floor again. "I thought we had something special."

"Get home safe," Joshua said dismissively, returning to his post.

Elias and Dakarai went through the glass doors and were spat back out into the rain. They stood there a moment, trying to let what just happened sink in. Dakarai took one look at Elias's disgruntled expression and burst out laughing. He clutched his sides and dabbed at his eye, though Elias couldn't tell if he was wiping away a tear or rain. That made him laugh.

Elias cleared his throat when their laughter became forced and trailed off.

"Well, I guess now we know he wasn't hitting on you before," Dakarai said, still holding on to his sides.

"Oh, you've got jokes," Elias said with a suck of his teeth. "Let's just get out of this rain. We don't need to water you anymore; you're tall enough."

He extended a hand to Dakarai, who took it and followed behind him in a renewed fit of giggles.

KAI

3:21 a.m.

CYPHR obviously was an unforgettable experience, but one thing that Kai had learned was that most things, if not everything, had a natural end. That went for the concert, for EZF as a complete group, and maybe for this night. What if it was only special because it was within the confines of such a short window of time? There was no telling how the two of them would feel in the morning, but he was excited to find out.

Kai and Elias joined hands and wound their way through the thicket of people outside smoking and chatting about the concert, not caring a single bit that they were getting soaked. Dodging plumes of smoke and those who had had a little too much to drink, the two boys came to many dead ends and false stops until they finally found a clearing. The rain refreshed their clothes, which clung to them in a mixture of sweat, confetti, and glitter. Kai didn't typically like the rain, but at times like this when it was warm, it was like he was a child again. He used to look at the weather on his parents' phones, and if it was going to rain, he'd put down pieces of cardboard in the mud. In the morning, he'd lift the cardboard and watch the earthworms wriggle back into the ground. He felt a little bit like those earthworms, satisfied at having answered to the vibrations of the raindrops beating down on the earth. However, even worms knew it was probably best to get the hell out of there before the sun came up.

Leaving the concert was disorienting, like stepping off a boat or getting out of a car after driving for hours. Everything just became aggressively normal and stationary once again. If not for the evidence all over their clothes, it might not have been that difficult to convince Kai that the entire night had never happened. It was almost eerie the way that attitudes can change with sound and with music and the atmosphere created by the people you choose to spend time with. To walk out of it almost made Kai sad. Elias, however, was the last vestige of the night, and admittedly, the best part of it.

The colors and the energy around Elias were somehow brighter as he lagged behind, wringing out his clothes as best he could. His aura rippled and crackled around him like flames, more intense than when they had first met.

Kai stopped for a moment to take a deep breath and collect his thoughts. When he looked back, Elias motioned to a convenience store across the street with bright lights and a flickering OPEN sign. The store was manned by a college kid who looked like they hadn't seen a customer in hours. They didn't even bother to act like they weren't playing on their phone when Kai and Elias went inside.

Kai pretended to deliberate over different brands of chips, but his eyes were fixed on Elias in the next aisle. Elias moved with purpose, as if he had been there before. That was one of his charms, his ability to command any space he was in. Elias was intense and imposing in a way, but it was backed up by a certain sensuality and patience that made it hard for Kai to believe that everyone in Elias's life had it out for him like he claimed. Yet, Kai had seen how a fight had almost unfolded at the show, and perhaps it was possible others simply felt threatened by Elias. However, that didn't mean Elias always had to engage.

Elias went to the checkout with several items in his hand, including a phone charger. He had a short conversation with the cashier as he paid, and they both looked in the same direction and pointed as though Elias was asking for directions. He gave the cashier a nod before rushing back toward Kai. He waved a hand in front of his face.

"You disappear into your mind again?" Elias asked, his voice low. "Take me with you next time?"

Kai smiled. Elias could be so sweet and attentive; he only wished Elias could extend some of that grace to himself.

Elias took Kai by the hand again and led him out of the store and a block over to a coin laundromat. There was no one inside when they went in, not even an employee. There were chairs and foldout tables, the plastic kind that his family sometimes rented for their reunions. A soda machine was the source of most of the light in the entire place since half of the panels on the ceiling had gone out. It was a small place with just one row of machines on each wall and aluminum tables for folding clothes in the middle.

Unsheathing his purchases from the convenience store, Elias let the plastic bag flutter to the floor, revealing two T-shirts that said I ♥ RALEIGH and two pairs of hibiscus-printed shorts clearly made for swimming.

"Don't say anything; it's all they had," Elias said, putting up a shushing hand.

"These probably would have been better before the rain," Kai joked.

176

"Oh, how silly of me. Let me get back into my time machine and give them to you two hours ago."

"While you're in the time machine, why don't you go back and *not* forget to take your keys out of the locker too?"

"And miss out on tonight? Nah, I'd rather throw my keys into the ocean."

Kai covered his mouth to hide his hot cheeks.

"Here," Elias said, handing Kai his new set of clothes. He then hooked a finger through one of Kai's belt loops and guided him to the small bathroom in the corner of the laundromat, pausing in front of the door.

"Just come in with me and save whatever line you were going to say for later," Kai said, holding open the door.

"I was going to offer to supervise you for safety," Elias said with a grin as he crossed in front of Kai.

Kai flicked on the light, which triggered a loud overhead vent, then closed the door behind them. Elias leaned against the tiled wall, his hands behind his back, staring Kai up and down. Kai turned toward the wall and, with a winding gesture of his hand, signaled for Elias to do the same.

A crop of goose bumps spread down Kai's back where he felt Elias's eyes on him. He hesitated but continued to shimmy out of his soaked shirt and shorts, which had been hanging on to his body like Saran Wrap. The sopping wet fabric fell to the floor like a ball of lead. He heard Elias's clothes fall with similar weight.

Turning his head to the side, Kai glanced out of the corner of his eye, catching only a glimpse of Elias's body as he pulled on his new T-shirt. Kai gulped hard and averted his eyes, refocusing on changing into his new outfit.

He looked in the mirror. *My first date after graduating high school, and this is what I'm wearing,* he thought. At least Elias would be wearing the same thing.

"You've got to be kidding me," Kai said when he turned to face Elias. He couldn't believe that Elias even looked good in this ridiculous outfit.

Elias wore a self-assured smile. "Are you trying to say I look good?"

"No, I'm not. Your head's already big enough."

"You like my big head."

"Yeah, whatever. Just give me your clothes."

Holding the ball of clothes out in front of him, as far from his body as he could, he exited the bathroom with Elias not far behind. He pulled air between his teeth, unwilling to show how winded he was from the accidental exercise. The heaviest thing he usually lifted was a paint brush.

Kai put their clothes into the mouth of a shiny chrome machine and clicked the door shut. Kai puzzled for a moment as he stared at the controls. *How complicated could this be?* he thought.

Elias took Kai by the shoulders, directing him to one of the tables in the middle of the room. A high-pitched clang echoed when Elias patted the surface, signaling for Kai to take a seat. "You trained me at work. Let me train *you* now," he said, and cracked a grin.

"How does everything you say sound so dirty? What you need is some home training."

Elias barked like a dog.

Kai massaged his cheeks, which were sore from all the smiling. He then leaned back and tried to pay attention to what Elias was doing with the machine, but his focus was pulled toward Elias's back and then down his arms.

"I only have two quarters, so seventeen minutes is all we get,"

Elias said over his shoulder. The coins dropped into the machine with a *chunk, chunk*.

The dryer kicked on, and Elias leaned against the table next to Kai, folding his arms. They talked for a while, but the late hour was finally catching up to them, and they settled into comfortable silence, watching their clothes spin. Several minutes passed. It wasn't until a loud growl came from Kai's stomach that they broke out of their shared daze.

"You're hungry?" Elias asked. He stood in front of Kai, leaning against his knees. "I can make you something when we get back."

"He cleans *and* he cooks?" Kai joked.

"Yes, he does," Elias replied. "How do you like your eggs in the morning?"

"I like them on someone else's plate. And it *is* the morning," Kai said, bopping his palm against Elias's forehead. Elias caught Kai's hand before he was able to bring it back to his side, delicately placing it on his chest. Elias's heart was beating fast beneath the red screen-printed heart of his T-shirt.

Being away from home, sleep-deprived, dressed like idiots—this was the perfect moment for Elias to kiss him. Kai had initiated both times tonight, and he yearned for Elias to take the lead here. As if reading his mind, Elias tilted Kai's head to the side and leaned in. But in the split second it would take for their lips to touch, the timer to the dryer went off, loud like a buzzer signaling the last moments of a basketball game.

Elias pretended he hadn't been startled by pacing around and trying to laugh it off, while Kai simply closed his eyes and shook his head.

Clearly sensing that the moment had passed, Elias said, "Let's go home."

29

ELIAS

4:01 a.m.

Elias went inside the bus station while Dakarai waited outside, leaning against a lamppost in the parking lot. Dakarai's phone illuminated his face as he checked his texts and voicemails.

Approaching the locker room, Elias placed his hand on the doorknob, almost certain that it would still be locked. However, to his surprise, when he pushed it, it opened, and a soft breeze invited him inside.

Unfolding his wallet as he located his locker, he dug around for the receipt and entered the code printed on it. Inside the bright red locker, his bag awaited him. It was just a messenger bag filled with a bunch of stuff he didn't even need, except for his house key. But then again, if he hadn't brought this big stupid bag—and if he had been smart enough to keep his house key in his pocket—the entire night never would have happened.

It was the first time in a long while where he could go out without worrying about whether his sister was home alone because his mom was at work, stressing about his mother eating something good after a twelve-hour shift, or being concerned about waking up early in the morning because he was always the one who had to get himself and William out of bed.

Yet, the freedom came with a sinking, guilty feeling, as if he was somehow leaving everyone behind. He had faulted William so much for doing the same thing, but there he was in Raleigh with a boy he liked at four in the morning. He hadn't slept a wink, there was barely any food in his fridge, he had work in only a few hours, and his bed wasn't even completely set up.

He threw the bag over his shoulder and rejoined Dakarai outside.

"Everything good?" Elias asked Dakarai as he approached, his house key dangling from his finger.

"Do we have to go back?" Dakarai asked as he picked at his hair. He had already loosened the braid that framed his face so much that it was unraveling. "My phone just started working again, and I have a million missed calls from my parents."

"Take my phone, then," Elias said, handing it to Dakarai. "Not a single person has checked up on me."

Dakarai abruptly got up, his and Elias's phones still in his grasp. Elias scrambled to follow him out into the parking lot. Broken glass and pebbles crunched under his feet as he ran to Dakarai, who had his arm cocked back, ready to launch both their phones into the trees.

"Hold up!" Elias shouted, grabbing Dakarai's arm just in time. He wrestled his phone from Dakarai's grasp and held it to his chest. His lungs were raw from the sprint. "You toss your own damn VCR. My phone's the one with the bus tickets."

Dakarai choked out a laugh. "Don't make me smile when I'm trying to be sad."

"When else would I make you smile?" Elias gently led Dakarai back to the bench. He slid himself up onto the armrest and motioned for Dakarai to come closer. Dakarai scooted over and rested his chin on Elias's leg. "What are you really mad at?"

Elias started on Dakarai's braid, unbraiding it and detangling with his fingers as best he could without the luxury of a comb or decent light.

"I think I'm glad Bobby's gone," he admitted.

Elias paused for a moment but then kept going. Separating the strands into three sections, he began redoing the braid.

Dakarai hugged on to Elias's leg as he continued, "If we'd gone to Berkeley together and been roommates, we would have only hung out with each other, and I would have never met you or anyone like you, for that matter."

Elias tied off the braid and pulled the rest of them back, securing them in a rubber band as they had been before. He took Dakarai's face in his hands. Dakarai tried to shrug him away, but there was nowhere for him to go. "There's no one like me."

Dakarai pushed his leg away and laughed. "Man, you know what I meant."

Returning the smile, Elias led Dakarai to the approaching bus. Hooking his finger into Dakarai's back pocket, he playfully pulled him backward as he went to board. "Me first," he joked, going ahead.

A chill ran up Elias's back and neck when Dakarai drew him in by the waist while the driver scanned his phone. His breathing became shallow, and he nervously picked at his polish-less nails as Dakarai wrapped his arms around him in a tight embrace. They waddled together, still connected, down the aisle of the bus and chose a spot toward the back.

Elias settled in first, immediately lifting the armrest between them. Dakarai leaned his cheek against Elias's hair as they waited for everyone else to take their seats.

KAI

5:15 a.m.

It didn't take long for the bus to fill up, and then the driver took his spot, and away they went. Kai absentmindedly stroked Elias's hair as the bus ticked along down the road toward home. Eventually, his eyes started to close. He was someone who could sleep almost anywhere, Bobby would say. If they were in the car, Kai was out within a minute. If they went to the movies, Bobby would always have to explain the end to him. If they were in class, Bobby had no choice but to wake him up because there was no way to cover up the sound of his snoring. This time, however, he tried to stay awake so Elias could get some sleep. He didn't mind; he felt rested just watching the way Elias slept peacefully against his chest.

    He found himself getting angry at the unevenness in the road and resentful of anyone around them who was talking too loudly. He used his arms to shield Elias from the overhead lights and tried to surround his body more in a weak attempt at blocking out some of the noise.

The bus station back home sat behind an abandoned restaurant. There was grass growing from every crack and crevice in the brick and concrete, and there was a full-grown tree that had broken through the windows. Despite it being the time for the sun to rise, the rainy weather from the night before persisted. The sky was still dark and the air muggy, lightly misting their skin as they zigzagged through the shared parking lot, dodging potholes and broken asphalt. Elias's eyes were barely open as he trudged along behind Kai. He had remained asleep throughout the entire ride.

It was only a short walk back to Moodie's shop, so without hesitation, Kai stooped low and gestured to his back, signaling for Elias to hop on. Apprehensively, Elias jumped up, and Kai hooked his arms around Elias's legs before straightening up and adjusting his weight. Elias slumped completely over Kai's shoulders, his light stubble creating a delicate abrasive sensation against his own cheek. The closeness and shared warmth of their skin made it hard to focus on anything else. Their clothes brushed against each other in movement.

"Do you think we'll make it to work today?" Kai asked.

"We're surrounded by caffeine. I think we'll manage," Elias replied, his morning voice low and husky, as he absentmindedly swung his legs.

The two continued along the charming Main Street. The converted row homes, made of brick, had cobblestone sidewalks that were uneven under their feet. Kai pointed out his favorite record store, where he used to spend time after school, a few places where he liked to people-watch and sketch, and the only other bookstore in town that Moodie considered competition.

It was his home, but it somehow looked different to him today, like he was seeing it in a new light.

ELIAS

5:58 a.m.

Back in New York, everything was loud but in a different way than it was in Moodie's little town. Of course, there were always cars and horns and people yelling in the street outside Elias's apartment. And the upstairs and downstairs neighbors and the ones to the left and right all had their specific noises that contributed to the soundtrack. But here, it was mostly crickets screeching into the night and loud whirring of industrial air-conditioning units. It wasn't like New York, where there were thousands of separate AC units and thousands of different voices and stomps and horns that made one unifying sound. It was like the separateness of each noise here made everything seem louder than all the collective noises put together.

From the way Dakarai spoke about his hometown, it was clear that he was in love with it, and it was becoming increasingly apparent why he had decided not to leave. Yet, Elias was still suspicious of how calm the town was and how peaceful it seemed. He didn't trust it.

"I guess the ride's over," Dakarai said as they approached the bookstore.

"Five more minutes," Elias protested, tightening his legs around Dakarai's waist to hold himself up.

"You're never beating the baby koala allegations," Dakarai joked. He then poked Elias between the ribs, and he immediately let go.

Digging through his bag for his keys, Elias handed them to Dakarai.

"Don't you think we're moving too fast?" Elias asked, folding his arms, his bottom lip poking out. Dakarai immediately started twisting his earring around. "I mean, I already gave you the key to my place."

Dakarai's shoulders relaxed. "We're outside and somehow you still manage to suck all the air out of the place," he teased.

"You talk too much for someone who can't breathe."

Elias wrapped his arms around Dakarai's middle and rested his head against his back as Dakarai continued to fumble with the ring of keys. Their attempts to be discreet were made futile by their hushed giggles.

They finally managed to open the door, nearly falling over each other in their rush to get into the store. Elias quickly closed and locked it behind them, sealing their barely suppressed laughter inside. Meanwhile, Dakarai ran to disarm the security system. The beeping from the keypad echoed in the empty bookstore.

The only light inside was the purple glow from the neon CLOSED sign on the window until Dakarai turned on the overhead ones.

Elias made himself comfortable in the manga section as Dakarai made himself useful in the staff room. Cross-legged on the floor, Elias thumbed through the seemingly infinite collection of plastic-sleeved issues neatly arranged on the red-cubed shelves. His eyes tracked Dakarai as he moved around, selecting a small batch of coffee beans from a private store in a cabinet only he could reach.

He put his nose to the bag and inhaled deeply, savoring the scent, before he loaded it into the grinder.

"I don't want a drink. I just want you," Elias said.

Dakarai subtly inspected him from the corner of his eye. "I'm making *myself* a drink."

Turning his attention back to the red shelves, Elias ran his fingers along the spines of the books until he stopped at one that caught his eye. Many of the others had women in sweeping landscapes as the background, colored in using all the brightest pantones. But this one was simple. It was all one color with only the silhouette of a man leaning against the side. Elias flipped it over, hoping that at least some of it would be in English, but the entire thing was written in Japanese.

He turned to Dakarai, who was tamping down coffee grounds into the portafilter in anticipation of an immaculately brewed espresso. "Dakarai," Elias called, "have you read this one?" He brandished the issue in the air.

Dakarai couldn't hear him over the pressurized sound of the water coursing through the machine. Elias smiled and returned to his manga, feigning interest in the pages while secretly watching Dakarai over the top with playful curiosity.

Dakarai's face was relaxed as fragrant dark liquid dripped into the glass demitasse. A hiss of steam filled the air as Dakarai frothed milk, his practiced hands creating art within the mug. With one hand underneath the saucer and a finger hooked into the handle of the mug, Dakarai finally closed the space between them. His presence seemed to expand as he neared. Elias adjusted his gaze to maintain eye contact.

"You really didn't make me anything?" Elias complained.

"This one is for you," Dakarai replied, setting the latte down and running back to the counter to retrieve the drink he'd made for himself outside of Elias's notice.

Elias thanked him with a wink. "Now will you tell me if you've read this manga?"

Dakarai eased onto the floor beside Elias, casually draping an arm over his shoulder and drawing him into an embrace.

"Can you translate it for me?" Elias asked, handing over the issue. His body seemed to lose all strength as he settled into the curve of Dakarai's arm. "Just a couple pages. I want to know what it's about."

The mug made a soft clink against the saucer as Dakarai set it down on the carpet, causing some of its contents to slosh over the side. His expression was indecipherable as he gazed down at the cover of the book and then flipped it to the back to read the summary. "Why this one? There are so many other books in the store that are written in your native language," Dakarai said. "I can recommend some other books for you."

Elias raised his brows, widening his eyes. "But I like this one."

"I don't think I can—"

"Please," Elias said, pushing the book farther into Dakarai's lap. "Just a few panels."

"I'll do my best."

Dakarai settled in more comfortably next to Elias. He folded his legs with the manga in his lap and turned to the first page, examining it for a while with a curious expression on his face. Elias's eyes followed the slope of Dakarai's nose, down his cupid's bow, all the way to his chin until his gaze rested on the tensed muscles of his neck.

Elias leaned in closer, hugging on to his arm and leaning his head onto Dakarai's shoulder for a better look as he cleared his throat and began. He pointed at each black-and-white panel, his fingers gliding down the words as he read them aloud. The pages revealed wooden houses crowned with dark-tiled roofs set against a canvas of rolling clouds and hills gilded in slender trees and winding rivers. The story was that of Yuto, the leader of a crime syndicate, who spends his days peacefully—nurturing a garden and gazing through sliding paper doors across the rice fields from his tatami mat in the fictional town of Hanakaze, Japan. On a business trip to Osaka, he would close the deal that would secure his future as the reigning leader of the entire region. He sits in a restaurant by himself, savoring fish over a steaming portion of rice while, unbeknownst to him, his bodyguards lie slain outside. In walks Hiroshi, an assassin for the rival crime syndicate led by the Nakamura family.

"For Yuto, it was love at first sight," Dakarai narrated. He took a sip of his neglected latte.

"There's romance in these things?" Elias asked, pointing to a panel.

"Yeah, of course, manga is full of romance."

Elias set his cup down, and with one deliberate motion, he reached over and turned the page for Dakarai. The slight rustle of the paper echoed in the otherwise quiet bookstore. "If this is a romance, then why is Hiroshi holding Yuto's heart?" He looked at Dakarai with a cutting glare. "You don't speak Japanese, do you?"

"That's what you get for trying to sell me that fake astrology chart earlier." Dakarai's words were nearly unintelligible through his laughter. Elias felt each chuckle in his own body. "I honestly thought you would catch on sooner," Dakarai said, holding his hands up in defense. Elias dug his elbow into Dakarai's side until he folded. "I'm sorry," he repeated over and over again, Elias continuing to nudge his ribs in their most ticklish spot.

"I was getting into it too. I was rooting for Yuto and Hiroshi. Are those even their real names?"

"I don't know." Dakarai was laughing so hard that it was barely audible—he was just vibrating with laughter, wiping tears away. Elias pushed him lightly in the chest. "We'll have to order the English translation into the store. I'll add it on to the next restock list for you."

They studied each other for a moment.

"Nah, it's all right," Elias said, pulling Dakarai toward him and back against his chest. "I like your version. Tell me the rest of it."

"Yuto's already dead, though," Dakarai replied.

"Use some creative license and bring his ass back."

"As much as I would like to bring Yuto back to life, Hiroshi needs to learn from his mistakes," Dakarai said, turning the page. "So Yuto stays very much dead, and Hiroshi decides to leave the assassin business for good. He moves to Tokyo, gets two cats, and works the rest of his life as a barista. The end."

"You've got to be kidding me. How do you go from ripping people's hearts out with your bare hands to serving iced Americanos in Tokyo?"

"People change."

"You really think people can change?"

"I think you could if you wanted," Dakarai replied. "Back at the show, you walked away from that fight. You talked a lot of shit before you walked away, but the point is that you did."

Elias smiled, embarrassed. "I was trying to protect you."

"You don't always have to protect everyone, you know," Dakarai said. "There are other ways to protect people without sacrificing yourself. I don't want to see you hurt, and neither should you."

Elias's chest tightened at Dakarai's words. He had always been the one to look after his family, and even now, he felt guilt for leaving them behind. But hadn't they been the ones to push him out? His thoughts drifted back to William's letter. *Maybe things weren't like this before, but now it feels like you're the one needing us more than we need you.* When had they stopped needing him? And why didn't they tell him?

He was thoughtful a moment before he said, "I know. I'll try."

Elias leaned his body into Dakarai, who nudged him in return, and they went back and forth, lightly pushing each other, swaying side to side as their shoulders touched. Elias yelled out in pain and then threw himself on the ground when Dakarai nudged him again. If being kicked off his high school team for poor sportsmanship taught him nothing else, he at least learned to fake a foul. Dakarai tried to pull Elias up by the arm, but he let his body go completely limp so that Dakarai had to support his entire weight like a rag doll. They couldn't stop laughing long enough to form coherent sentences. Soon after, Dakarai gave up entirely.

Silhouetted by the fluorescent lights above, he leaned over Elias, his face unchanging. The rough carpet fibers irritated Elias's skin even through his shirt, yet he made no attempt to escape the cage of Dakarai's arms. Protected by Dakarai's shadow, Elias slowly unshielded his eyes, yet his arms felt awkward lying useless by his sides. He reached for something, anything he could put between him and Dakarai, but he only grasped floor. Elias settled on Dakarai's forearm; his own heartbeat pulsed in his fingertips as he traced his thumb along a vein.

"We have work in three hours" was the only thing Elias could think to say.

Dakarai leaned in, the chain of his crystal necklace draping onto Elias's chest. "Should we try to get some sleep?"

Elias's heartbeat was loud in his ears. "I won't be able to sleep."

"Me either." Dakarai answered so quickly that Elias wasn't even sure if he had spoken.

"Can I make you breakfast?" Elias asked, still running his thumb along Dakarai's forearm.

"Are you inviting me upstairs?" Dakarai's pupils trembled as he searched Elias's face for his intention.

"Yes, but I need, like, two minutes to tidy up first."

"How did you make a mess already?" he scolded. "It's barely been two days yet."

"I've been living out of my suitcases."

"You didn't think you'd stay?"

"I don't know."

"What about now?"

"I guess it's not so bad here," Elias said with a begrudging smile. "Now, are you going to let me up, or we going to stay like this until it's time to open?" Dakarai drew a deep preparatory breath but didn't move. "I mean, we can stay here. It's fine by me." Elias pulled Dakarai by the chain toward his puckered lips.

The two laughed together, causing a sudden shift in the mood as they remembered where they were. Rising to their feet, they exchanged barely concealed glances, each dusting off and smoothing out their clothing as if to brush off the lingering tension that hung in the air around them.

"You know I don't care how your place looks," Dakarai said.

Elias blocked Dakarai's path, but Dakarai persisted, steadily advancing and cornering him against the wall. Something dug into Elias's shoulder blade, but Dakarai prevented him from looking with a firm grip on the back of his neck. The two stared at each other for a moment, each wondering what the other would do next.

Dakarai blinked rapidly, his gaze firmly fixed on Elias's mouth. Elias slid his hand down to the side of Dakarai's face. He held him like that, unmoving, until he felt a swallow beneath his palm. He flinched, and a sharp pain immediately shot through his shoulder blade. The plastic door to the security keypad fell to the ground with a bounce.

Dakarai let out an airy laugh. "Just as I thought—all bark, no bite."

Elias smiled, embarassed. "Just give me, like, two minutes," he said, replacing the covering to the keypad.

"I'll clean up down here. I'll see you in *one* minute," Dakarai said, stooping to collect their cold coffees.

Elias nodded slowly as he edged away, colliding with the wall again. He waited until he was concealed behind the door of the staircase leading up to his apartment before rubbing his aching shoulder.

He took the steps in twos, dashing into his apartment to smooth out his bedspread and hide his suitcases in the closet.

KAI

6:43 a.m.

Of course, Kai had always known about the studio apartment above the shop, but he'd never had a reason to go up there. It had been vacant since he met Uncle Moodie, and only about a day before Elias arrived, the windows were boarded up to prevent break-ins and storm damage.

At the top of the stairs, the door to the apartment was open. Elias stuck his head out, a lazy, sideways smile spread across his face.

"What is it like looking up at me for a change?" he asked.

"It's not bad," Kai replied, his cheeks getting hot.

As Kai climbed the stairs to Elias's apartment, he became acutely aware of his breathing. The concrete walls sequestered the sound, and his footsteps were thunderous as they pressed down on the creaky wooden treads that dipped in the centers. He considered turning around and going home. After all, this was his coworker—someone he'd have to see every day. His boss's nephew, no less. He risked blowing up his entire life. But then again, not all changes were bad.

Elias stood at the top of the stairs, waiting. Backlit by the warm glow of his apartment and the neon purple shining through the singular window, only Elias's silhouette was visible. He was self-conscious of the amount of noise his footsteps were making. He sped up to get it over with but then slowed down as not to seem too eager. Blood coursed through his ears. Attempting to conceal his anxiety, he thrust his hands into his pockets. However, he nearly stumbled and had to withdraw them to steady himself against the wall.

"That was almost a season ender," Elias joked with a low melodic laugh. He looked up at Kai, not moving his head, only his eyes, as he pulled him the rest of the way into the apartment.

Kai bit his lip. They'd been alone all night, but this kind of alone, with a door closed behind them, was the first time they were truly in private.

Elias pointed to his right and said, "Living room," then to his left and said, "Dining room," and then behind him and said, "Bathroom." Then he pulled Kai by the arm into the kitchen, which was only partially separated from the rest of the studio apartment by a partition wall with a small serving hatch. "And I don't think I have to tell you what this room is called." He then walked to the other side of the apartment and threw himself onto the bed. It was only a mattress on the floor, with the duvet and pillows hastily thrown over. "And here's my bed," Elias said with a grin.

"Behave," Kai replied. "It's cute," he added, looking around. "Small, but cute."

It wasn't that Kai was expecting Elias to be messy, but he wasn't expecting him to be this neat either. Even his curtains looked like they might have been ironed or steamed; there wasn't a crease in sight. It reminded him of Bobby, who organized his closet by season, then fabric, and then color. Kai shook his head and let out a small chuckle. Bobby was, after all, his first crush, so it appeared Kai had a type.

Kai leaned back, propping his weight against the ledge of the serving hatch, observing Elias as he sifted through the fridge. Elias reached for a carton of eggs, then hesitated and withdrew. He repeated the process with the cheese. A laugh escaped Kai, capturing Elias's attention.

Elias took a few timid steps toward Kai. "Don't worry, I'll feed you, but can I make a suggestion first?"

"Don't ask permission."

Elias stepped even closer, and Kai's entire body stiffened. "I think you should let me kiss you now so we don't spend the rest of the morning thinking about it."

Kai's eyebrows rose so far they almost left his face entirely. "Why would I be thinking about it?"

"Because we're alone, this apartment only has one room, so we're technically in my bedroom, and I'm about to cook for you. Trust me, you're going to be thinking about it."

"And what about you?" Kai asked with a playful nudge.

Elias leaned in closer. "I've *been* thinking about it. I thought I was pretty clear about that."

There was a long stretch of silence. Elias stood unblinking; his mouth flickered with what Kai would have believed was annoyance yesterday but what he now knew was amusement or perhaps intrigue.

Although he wanted to feel Elias's lips on his again, he finally said, "I'm not going to let you kiss me. We're just going to have to think about it all morning. Maybe even all day at work."

Elias's mouth dropped open in surprise. "It's like that?"

"It's like that."

Elias crinkled his nose and said, "I didn't really want to kiss you anyway."

"Oh yeah?" Kai said, raising an eyebrow. "Because there are cameras downstairs, so you've been caught in at least 720p lying your ass off."

They stood like this for a few moments, watching each other, each waiting for the other to act. The tension broke, however, when Kai's phone started ringing, just out of reach of his fingertips. Elias dropped his head, his eyes fixed on the floor. Kai put some distance between them, but Elias swiftly reached out, catching Kai's wrist before he could fully retreat. He sat him down on one of the high barstools and said, "If that's Bobby, don't answer it."

Kai narrowed his eyes. "He called when my phone wasn't working. I should let him know I'm safe."

"It's the middle of the night in his time zone. It can't wait until the morning?"

"You don't have to be jealous of him, you know. We're only friends, and he has a girlfriend."

Elias didn't respond. He just started moving around the kitchen, preparing breakfast with a silent determination.

It was clear that Kai had made the right choice in having Elias primarily run the café portion of the shop, because everything he did seemed so natural. His timing was always on point, so he was never standing around looking confused. By the time the bread clicked out of the toaster, Elias already had the cutting boards and tools he used washed, avocados sliced, and shakers of salt and red pepper flakes ready to go. He set the plate down in front of Kai. Taking a seat next to him, he dragged his stool closer by the foot spindle.

Kai took a bite and turned his attention back to Elias, who was still watching him through hooded eyes. "Are you going to stare at me the whole time?"

Elias wet his lips and appeared thoughtful for a moment. "I'm thinking of what to say to you. You just happen to be sitting in my thinking place."

Kai shook his head and took another satisfying crunch of toast. "I'm listening."

"I . . ." Elias began but then appeared to reconsider his words. "You know what? Just forget it," he said, the same coldness from when they first met making a sudden return—when he wouldn't even look at Kai while handing him the tissue.

The wooden floors creaked beneath his feet as he swiftly moved around the kitchen, gathering the ingredients to prepare a plate for himself. With Kai at his back, all that resonated in the air was the rhythmic sound of Elias's knife gliding across the cutting board. Kai wrapped his arms around Elias's waist and pulled him into a back hug but was immediately rebuffed.

Abruptly slamming the knife down, Elias let out an exasperated breath and spun toward Kai. "What am I doing? Why am I treating you like this?" he muttered, more to himself than to Kai. "All night, all I've wanted is your attention. And when I didn't have it, I just wanted to"—he turned Kai's head to face him—"start screaming until you looked at me." He took a deep breath. "You say you want to be in a relationship, but are you aware that you're already in one with your best friend?"

Kai blinked hard, trying to process what he'd just heard. *A relationship with Bobby?* Of course he was in a relationship with Bobby. A friendship. Kai had made that clear plenty of times throughout the night.

Kai and Elias grew quiet for a moment. Elias fiddled with the hem of his shorts, picking at some of the threads on the bottom with his fingernails as he avoided Kai's eyes. He then gathered himself and looked directly into Kai's gaze. Elias, his skin slick with sweat, was even more beautiful than usual, shining like Carolina Gold. "I get that you guys are close," he said. "Trust me, it's a huge green flag that you have such a good friend. But you guys kissed when you were kids, and even though it didn't mean anything, you broke a barrier between friendship and romance, and now it seems like you're somewhere in between. Which is okay if you're both aware and intentional about it, but it doesn't seem to me like you are. Every time you play flirt or call each other your little pet names, you just make it impossible to set boundaries. Do you not see that? If you don't make space for other people, everyone you date is only ever going to be a fling as long as you have this Bobby kid waiting at home for you. But he isn't home anymore, Kai. You chose to be apart from him. He's gone, so you need to let him be gone," Elias said, leaning over the counter.

Kai squirmed under Elias's unyielding stare. Elias hadn't been this serious about anything all night. He'd even called him *Kai* for the first time. Kai's lip twitched, unsure of what to say. "Are you really jealous?" was all that came out.

Elias's jaw tightened. "Damn right I'm jealous."

Is this really jealousy, or is it ego? Kai wondered, studying Elias's face. Elias was constantly sizing himself up against others; he had felt threatened by Bobby's intelligence earlier in the night, and it was clear that Kai gave Elias a bit of a Napoleon complex. But had Kai misread the situation? Could it be that Elias had been truly jealous all along simply because he liked Kai?

"I'm right here with you," Kai said, sliding his phone across the counter. "But you've let me make all the first moves tonight. If you want my attention, then what are you going to do about it?" He held Elias's gaze, as if he was issuing a challenge. "Well?"

"I'm waiting on you."

"Waiting on me for what?"

Elias let out a breath. "If you make me stand on my tiptoes, I'll never forgive you."

Kai's belief was confirmed—it had only ever been about Elias's ego.

"Then you don't really want it," Kai said, defeated.

"I do," Elias replied, determined.

"No, you don't."

"I do."

"Then do it."

"Fine."

Elias was suddenly at eye level, and before Kai could register what was happening, Elias's lips were on his. It took a moment for Kai to get over the initial shock, but soon he was kissing him back. Elias seized the drawstrings of Kai's ridiculous hibiscus board shorts and pulled, gasping as the edge of the counter pressed into his back. Kai swiftly hoisted Elias onto the counter by the waist, their connection unbroken. In that instant, Kai had never been so glad to be wrong, as the current of the moment surged between them, taking him back to their first touch, when Elias's aura burned bloodred.

Kai cradled Elias's face in his hand, and Elias nuzzled into it, planting a soft kiss on his palm before returning to his lips.

This is happening, Kai's mind screamed. As he finally relaxed and accepted the fact that Elias's feelings for him were genuine, the beep of the alarm keypad downstairs sounded, and they abruptly broke apart, eyes wide.

"Oh, what now?" Kai whined.

ELIAS

7:02 a.m.

Elias clenched his fists and launched into a silent rage, punching the air and letting out a whisper yell. "What's Moodie doing here?" he fumed.

"Your clumsy ass must have triggered the panic button when you knocked into the keypad!" Dakarai responded.

"*Shh!*" Elias clapped his hand over Dakarai's mouth.

He slapped Elias's hand away. "You *shh*."

Elias persisted, attempting to cover Dakarai's mouth once more, culminating in a struggle until both raised their arms in surrender.

"I'll go apologize to him. It's not that big of a deal," Dakarai whispered.

"No," Elias said, wrinkling his nose in disgust. "I can't let him know I'm the one who set off the alarm, and I for sure don't want him knowing you're here. He had, like, five rules, and I'm pretty sure I broke every single one of them. He'll send me back to New York in a heartbeat, and I finally want to be here."

The nervous energy was evident in Dakarai as he repeatedly ran his hands over his braids, seeming to find comfort in the texture. He froze when the first step up to the apartment creaked. In one movement, he shut off the lights and pulled Elias down with him. The two sat next to each other on the kitchen floor beneath the breakfast bar, as though bracing for an earthquake.

The sound of Moodie's heavy steps echoed up the stairway, becoming more apprehensive the closer they got, until they stopped altogether. "Eli, you there?" His voice was low but clear through the solid oak door. Elias kept his eyes purposefully shut, punctuating each syllable of Moodie's words with a teeth grind. "Are you in there, nephew?" Moodie asked. "Did you set off the store alarm?"

Still, Elias didn't answer. There was a long sigh on the other side of the door, followed by fading footsteps as they moved away. The jingle of the front door didn't make a sound as they expected, however. Beneath them, the muffled creaks of floorboards and the shuffling of Moodie's feet told the boys everywhere he went— from the counter to the back shelves, to the break room, and to the bathroom twice. About half an hour went by, and Elias remained stoic, his hand grasped firmly on Dakarai's knee.

"I shouldn't have shut off the lights," Dakarai said in a hushed voice. "We can't even turn them back on now or Moodie will know you've been up here hiding from him."

Elias opened his eye a sliver. Only the outline of Dakarai's silhouette was visible as slats of meager light from the streetlamps filtered in through the barred window on the unusually dark morning. It may as well have been the middle of the night. Giving Dakarai's knee a comforting squeeze, he murmured softly, "I'm good. It's about time I got over this stupid fear anyway."

At once, Dakarai's leg moved from beneath his hold, and a flash of red shone through his eyelids. He opened his eyes to find that Dakarai had kicked open the fridge door, allowing light to spill out onto the kitchen floor. It wasn't bright enough to light the entire room, but it offered a golden glow, enough for them to see each other at least. There was a subtle resonance in Elias's chest.

Dakarai settled in beside Elias once more. The two sat shoulder to shoulder against the wall with their arms relaxed at their sides.

Elias pulled Dakarai close by the front of his shirt. Dakarai's breath shook as they lingered there, just inches apart. His eyes flickered to Elias's lips, then back up to his eyes before he placed a light, chaste kiss on the corner of Elias's mouth. There wasn't a single thought in Elias's head as he pulled Dakarai into another dizzying kiss. It didn't matter whether Moodie was downstairs or not. They'd just have to be quiet. He wasn't sure if minutes or hours were going by. He didn't care that the floor was hard and cold or that his back would likely hurt all day. Nothing. He'd always been embarrassed by his fear of the dark, but with Dakarai, he couldn't feel ashamed even if he tried. He felt like he could just exist.

Gasping against Dakarai's mouth as Dakarai's chest rose and fell, he didn't want to stop, but he needed just a moment to catch his breath. He began to pull away, but Dakarai made a noise of protest, not allowing the retreat. Elias put a finger to his lips. *Shh.*

He sat back with an exhale of relief, his attention fixed on the wall, the only thing keeping him upright.

The moment had reduced him to his most base desires, and all he could focus on was his empty stomach. Still in a daze, he reached over his head to the counter above, grabbing Dakarai's unfinished breakfast. With a resounding crunch, he snorted with laughter, scattering crumbs. "What? I'm starving," he whispered with a gulp. "You ate, but I didn't get a chance yet."

Dakarai hooked Elias behind the knee and pulled him closer. "Because you were busy staring at me."

"No, I wasn't."

"Yes, you—"

Elias stopped him mid-sentence with a bite of toast. Dakarai's cheeks puffed up like a squirrel as he tried to chew and suppress a laugh at the same time. Elias found his gaze fixed on his mouth, observing its movement as he chewed. "My mother would have a fit if she saw the fridge open like this. *Do you pay bills in here?*" Elias said in a mocking tone. Dakarai moved to close the door, but Elias stopped him.

Elias had his legs folded, completely leaning into the curve of Dakarai's arm, with his entire body weight resting against Dakarai's chest as they joked and ate. Dakarai kept a protective arm across Elias's chest, clutching his shirt to maintain the position. Elias, taking advantage of the situation, fed himself and then reached over his shoulder to feed Dakarai as well.

"You know, to this day, my own parents have never even made me a vegan meal. Intentionally," Dakarai said under his breath.

An unexpected knock echoed through the room, and Elias's throat tightened; a choking fit ensued. He sipped his water, shutting his eyes and shaking his head, a flush of embarrassment warming his cheeks. "I swear he's like the embodiment of a cold shower," he groaned.

"I can hear you," Moodie's voice sounded through the door. "This is your last chance to get out here or I'll have to watch the security footage and see what kind of trouble you've been getting into."

"We do *not* need him seeing what kind of trouble we've been getting into," Dakarai whispered, the urgency thick in his voice. "Go talk him down."

"I'm going," Elias said. "But think about what I said earlier, all right?"

KAI

7:18 a.m.

The air was warm and fragrant as Kai stood beside one of the open windows. Sweetgum trees lined the herringbone-patterned sidewalks, shading the street with a verdant canopy. One stood tall before him, its prickly gumballs rustling in the breeze. Pale light streamed through its star-shaped leaves as the clouds started to subside.

Left alone in the apartment, Kai regarded the few possessions scattered around the studio. Some black T-shirts hung on the back of a chair by the window. He had half a mind to poke around some of Elias's bags to see if he really was who he said. The bags were probably full of passports with different names on them. He wouldn't have been surprised if he were some kind of spy, given his good looks.

Kai peered through the window again at the sweetgum leaves. Maybe its star-shaped leaves were a symbol of the celestial and the divine. But then again, it could just be a leaf. Elias could be his twin flame, or he could just be a boy that Kai liked right now, in this moment only, the way Bobby had been.

Back then, Kai's crush on Bobby made a lot of sense. He was

cute—they got along so well that they barely even needed to talk to know what the other was thinking, and things with him were just easy. It wasn't until years later, when they got to high school, that Kai realized he was in the majority—almost everyone who met Bobby fell in love with him. Then, after he and Bobby kissed, Kai realized they were nothing more than friends—platonic soulmates, really.

He thought about texting Bobby, but maybe they didn't have to update each other every second of the day. It'd be nice to catch up over thumbprint cookies and matcha lattes when Bobby came back for Thanksgiving.

Maybe Elias had a point. He'd been so serious, and Elias wasn't the type to let himself be vulnerable like that unless he meant it—going so far as to admit his jealousy. It'd be unfair of Kai to not at least entertain the idea that he had been treating Bobby as a placeholder. But it wasn't as Elias thought. It wasn't because of their kiss or their pet names. It was something much simpler than that. All the times Kai had fallen in love, he'd routinely scared off the other person. They'd try to spare his feelings with a lie—needing to move abruptly, picking up a far-fetched hobby. But maybe, just maybe, Kai kept trying because of what came after. At first, his motivation was to experience a great love. But perhaps over time, as he'd get his heart smashed again and again, it became more about how good it felt to cry on Bobby's shoulder. Bobby would tell him to stop believing in the stars, but he wouldn't challenge him—not really, anyway. If he'd gone with Bobby to Berkeley, that cycle would be all he'd ever know. Deep down, Kai understood that.

For all of Bobby's explaining, he'd never managed to shake Kai's beliefs—not in the way Elias had. And Elias had done so by affirming them. For the first time, Kai didn't want to rush to the part where he'd end up on his living room floor playing video games with Bobby. Even if he did, Bobby wouldn't be there now. If Kai hadn't been so eager to fast-track his heartbreak five years ago, not even waiting for Elias to reject him at the park, they could've had each other in their lives all this time.

At the sound of Moodie and Elias nearing the door, Kai acrobatically leapt over the back of the couch, executing a mid-air spin before gracefully landing in a lounging position. Folding his hands over his stomach, he closed his eyes, feigning nonchalance. After a few moments, he sneakily peeked through the blurred slit of one eye, only to find the door still securely closed.

"Why the hell am I pretending to sleep? I'm not faking sick to stay home from school," Kai muttered to himself.

Yet, when the voices in the stairway swelled again, he snapped his eyes shut and seamed his lips once more.

ELIAS

7:18 a.m.

The judgmental eyes of Uncle Moodie awaited Elias in the stairway. Disappointment transformed Moodie's face into Elias's mother's—finally revealing the familial likeness.

Walking past Moodie, Elias leaned against the cold brick wall, folding his arms over his chest. *I guess it's a good thing I never unpacked; even my avocados lasted longer here than I did,* he thought.

More of a statement than a question, Moodie said, "You were out all night, huh?" eliciting an affirming nod from Elias. Frustrated, Moodie pinched the bridge of his nose, closing his eyes for a moment before finally saying, "We're family. Do you know what that means?"

"That we're stuck together?"

"You think I talk to my sister every day because we're stuck together? Look, I didn't choose to be an uncle, much less yours. What I did choose, though, was letting you live here because of your mother. You deliberately breaking my rules tells me that you don't want anything to do with me—you just want to go home. If that's your choice, then that's fine; we're not *stuck together*. But you need to know that I want you here. I think you're a good kid—"

"*Pft.* No, you don't. You made that completely clear to me."

Moodie took a deep breath. "Did you fix the dessert case?" he asked, and Elias nodded, caught off guard by the unexpected question. "I'm realizing that I only know what your mother tells me about you. She says you get into fights. That you don't listen to her. That you don't listen to anybody."

Elias let out an incredulous snort.

"Something funny?" Moodie asked.

"I'm sorry, but what is there to listen to?" Elias replied. "The only time she talks to me is when she's telling me to watch Nia or take out the trash or do whatever the hell else Dad used to do around the house. It's either that or she's complaining about him, even though I keep telling her I don't want to hear it. Dad does the same thing. And they both let William do whatever he wants, and I'm stuck having to listen to it."

Taking a step closer, Moodie placed a hand on Elias's shoulder. "To be honest, Eli," he began, and Elias was tempted to correct him on the nickname, but in the moment, he didn't mind it as much. Moodie continued, "I'm surprised by the young man you've become. You take on a lot of responsibility, and you care more than you like to show. I get that it can be frustrating when people don't see that." Elias was having a hard time meeting Moodie's eyes, but he could feel his gaze on him as he leaned in closer to say, "You can forget about all the rules. I want you to be comfortable here. But can you just promise me that you'll try to see things from your parents' perspective? I'm not saying that they haven't made mistakes. But you're grown now, and maybe your relationship with them can grow too. You're mature enough to decide what relationships you want to have in your life. That goes for your parents, me, your brother and sister, *and* who you choose to date."

Finally lifting his eyes to meet Moodie's, Elias asked, "You mean Dakarai? I thought you wanted me to stay away from him. That's the reason you even came up with all these crazy rules in the first place."

"Like I said, you're old enough to make your own decisions. And now that I've heard your side of things, I trust you'll make good ones."

"This is— I lowkey thought you just had a problem with me dating boys," Elias said.

"I don't have a problem with you dating boys. I have a problem with that hard head of yours."

Elias's mouth dropped open in indignation but slowly softened into a smile.

Moodie continued, "I hope you use this as an opportunity to figure some things out. And I don't mean you have to plan out your entire future. But do you think you know what your next step is?"

Elias's tone softened. "I think I want to talk to my brother."

"You're a good man, Eli," Moodie replied, smiling warmly. Again, Elias decided not to correct him on the name. It annoyed him every time his brother, sister, and parents used it, but perhaps Moodie had earned the right to annoy him too.

Moodie wrapped his arms around Elias's shoulders and delivered one sharp pat to his back as if trying to dislodge food from his throat. The hug was over before Elias even got a chance to participate in it; his arms remained hanging uselessly at his sides.

"You're a back patter, Mood," Elias said dryly.

"Shut up," Moodie said, releasing him. "Now, go get some rest. Take the day off. I'll work with Kai today."

"No, Dakarai and I will—" Elias pulled his lips between his teeth and exhaled deeply. His eyes flickered to the apartment door before he had a chance to stop himself.

Moodie trailed Elias's gaze. "Is Kai in there?" His eyes lingered on the door, but then he swiftly lifted his hands in a gesture of surrender. "Actually, that's none of my concern."

"I'll work with Dakarai today," Elias said, his cheeks getting hot.

"Teenagers," Moodie mused. "I'm not built for this." He then headed toward the stairs.

"Wait," Elias said. Moodie raised a questioning eyebrow. "Could I... Can I come over for dinner later?"

"Food tastes better when someone else makes it for you, doesn't it?"

"Don't get all sentimental on me, Mood. I'll come over after we close."

With a warm smile, Moodie left without another word.

When Elias reentered the apartment, Dakarai was fast asleep on the couch. He snored and rolled over, one of his legs falling to the ground with a thud. Elias froze like a statue, waiting to see if Dakarai would wake up. But he simply readjusted his position and continued snoring. Elias moved to the couch, gently lifting Dakarai's leg back up and covering it with the blanket from his bed.

Tiptoeing to the bathroom, he shut the door as quietly as he could. He leaned over the sink, bringing his face just inches away from his reflection, and gave his tired eyes a rough rub with his palms, making himself wince. Touching his fingers to the tops of his cheekbones, he was comforted by the fact that it didn't hurt much anymore. Lowering the toilet seat, Elias sat down and let out a deep sigh. He turned on the faucet so Dakarai couldn't hear his fidgeting, as every movement made the rickety toilet seat creak.

There had been so many moments all night when the two of them could have turned back, but they just kept stepping over the line every time they drew a new one. Maybe Moodie had been right to tell him to stay away from Dakarai, but it already felt too late.

There was just something about Dakarai that reminded him of a very specific time in his life, one he didn't often think about. It was from when he was a child before Nia was born. When he and his parents would walk around the city, they always held his hand and had him walk on the inside of the sidewalk, where it was safer. Yet, somewhere along the way, the dynamics shifted. Elias found himself always being the one on the outside. It wasn't until tonight that he realized that he missed the simplicity of just holding on to someone's hand, shutting off his brain, and trusting them to take him wherever he needed to be. Now that he'd been reminded of this feeling, he never wanted to be without it again. He'd let Dakarai stay in Raleigh with him for a reason, even though it felt more natural for Elias to tell Dakarai to go.

Elias flicked off the bathroom light and stepped quietly back into his apartment. Dakarai was still sleeping soundly, but he stirred as Elias knelt beside him. He studied Dakarai's face as he opened his eyes.

KAI

7:45 a.m.

Kai scooted toward the edge of the couch, leaving a space on the inside. Elias maneuvered over him, nestling into the snug spot. As they settled, their gazes met, lying close, face-to-face. The limited space and shared body heat and breath created an unseen thread between them.

Kai signaled for Elias to come closer. His body was jerky and awkward as he leaned his head against Kai's chest. "How was your talk with Mood?" he whispered, rubbing Elias's arm up and down with his thumb.

"Good. Really good, actually," Elias replied as he idly played with the crystal on Kai's necklace.

"He's a good dude. And," Elias said as a nervous laugh escaped his lips, "I think he gave us his blessing."

"His blessing," Kai repeated. He smiled, charmed by Elias's sudden shyness. "His blessing to do what?"

Elias traced his thumb over the small crevice beneath Kai's pinkie and said, "To see if I'm that little line on your palm," before firmly intertwining their fingers.

Sleepily, Kai asked, "Is that what you want?"

"I don't know," Elias replied honestly, "but will you give me a chance anyway?"

They lay there holding hands for a moment before Elias reached up and placed a sweet kiss on Kai's lips. The two kissed lazily as their bodies jumbled together on the couch that was way too small for them. Knotted up in each other, they eventually fell asleep.

9:42 a.m.

Hours later, Kai was jolted awake by his ringing phone. He tumbled off the couch, and his tailbone beat the rest of his body to the ground. He quickly scrambled to his feet and searched for Elias in the room. To his relief, Elias wasn't there, but to his disappointment, Elias wasn't there.

Kai's heart did a flip when he saw Elias's name on his caller ID. He steeled his nerves and cleared his throat a few times before answering.

"Hello?" His voice cracked. "Shit."

A low melodic voice laughed on the other side of the line. "I was going to text but didn't think you had texting on that fax machine you been calling a phone."

"Ha. Ha," Kai said dryly. "The joke's on you because I like calling better than texting."

"I figured. Anyway, I thought I'd let you sleep. I opened up the store. Come down when you're ready."

Kai splashed water on his face and rubbed some toothpaste on his teeth so he could at least try to look somewhat presentable at work. His eyes were half closed, and he nearly had to stand on the toilet to allow enough room for the door to shut.

When he entered the bookstore, he was met with a CYPHR song he'd never heard before. *The exclusive track,* Kai thought warmly.

Elias was sitting on the counter playing with his phone. It was a mystery how Elias managed to look so good in the morning. Kai resembled something that was pulled out of a hairbrush, but Elias was in all black looking like someone who would promise to bring your daughter home at 10:00 p.m. but not specify what day.

Elias smiled when he noticed Kai.

"Good morning," he said after a beat. "Did you sleep well?"

"I always do," Kai sang. "Did *you?*"

"Nope. Never do." Elias hopped off the counter. "Good talk," he said, giving Kai a few soft taps on the cheek. "Now, let's go have a company meeting." He took Kai's hand and began leading him to the storage room.

Kai swatted him off. "What about the store?"

"Union break. Fifteen minutes."

Kai glanced around, taking in the darkened shopkeeper's bell above the door, the mismatched tables and chairs in the café, the bright yellow and green velvet couches in the reading nook, and finally, the rows and rows of comics reaching almost to the ceiling. The mural he'd painted cast a colorful light on the books, almost like church windows.

His eyes rested on that particular spot in the manga section, and he said, "Five minutes."

"Fifteen minutes," Elias replied without hesitation.

"This isn't a debate," Kai said, his mouth dropping open in disbelief at Elias's audacity.

"Ten."

Kai stroked the stubble of his chin with his thumb as he looked Elias up and down. "Deal. Let's go."

Elias walked ahead, pausing in the doorframe before disappearing into the back room.

I just wanted to go to a concert with my friends, Kai thought as he followed.

Was it a mistake to start something romantic with his coworker, a coworker he'd have to see almost every single day? The nephew of his boss, no less? Most likely. Probably almost certainly. But the mistake was already made, and he wasn't taking it back.

ACKNOWLEDGMENTS

In my last book, *Rules for Rule Breaking*, my darling debut, I thanked myself. I've experienced no meaningful character development since then, so first and foremost, I'd like to thank myself again.

Thank you to my wonderful agent, Jim McCarthy. To my editor, Joanna Cárdenas, the true star of this book, who is stuck with me for as long as she'll have me. All the thanks in the world to Namrata Tripathi and the entire Kokila fam for always having my back. Bex Glendining, you really ate down with this cover art. Thank you, Kaitlin Yang, for the cover design, and Asiya Ahmed, for the inside design (but also for inspiring me to rewrite the rain scenes).

I'd like to express my utmost appreciation for SUGA/Min Yoongi/Agust D, without whom the idea for this book would not exist. I'd also like to thank the two people who bought their Agust D concert tickets from me the morning of the show, allowing me to buy new tickets and sit closer to Yoongi while he had one of my favorite haircuts to date. Since that concert, I've headcanoned that you two are in a relationship, so I'll be expecting my invite to the wedding in the mail.

I have to mention my two cats, Minju and Lady J, the loves of my life. One, because Lady J is currently sitting on my legs and I have no feeling from the knees down. But two, because I nearly lost Minju this year and I reached my final form as a cat butler caring for her for the last seven months. We're not totally out of the woods yet, but we'll get there!

I'd write a full love letter to Dakarai and Elias if I had the time (and space), but I think I already did with this book. The way I talk about you both, it's like you're my children. Thank you for being so adorable, but you better not stay out all night without calling again.

Lastly, I'd like to acknowledge my family and friends. Consider yourselves acknowledged. I'll see you in the next one!